SHANNON: THE ROAD TO WHISKEY CREEK

A Sheriff Shannon Western

Other books by Charles E. Friend:

Shannon's Law
Shannon's Way
Shannon: U.S. Marshal
Shannon: Carrying the Star
Shannon's Ride

SHANNON:
THE ROAD TO
WHISKEY CREEK

A Sheriff Shannon Western

•

Charles E. Friend

Gloucester Library
P.O. Box 2380
Gloucester, VA 23061

AVALON BOOKS
NEW YORK

Published by Thomas Bouregy & Co., Inc.
160 Madison Avenue, New York, NY 10016

Library of Congress Cataloging-in-Publication Data

Friend, Charles E.
  Shannon : the road to Whiskey Creek / Charles E. Friend.
    p. cm.
  ISBN 0-8034-9780-6 (acid-free paper)
1. Shannon, Clay (Fictitious character)—Fiction. 2. United States marshals—Fiction. I. Title.

PS3556.R5663S387 2006
813'.54—dc22
                                        2005033808

PRINTED IN THE UNITED STATES OF AMERICA
ON ACID-FREE PAPER
BY HADDON CRAFTSMEN, BLOOMSBURG, PENNSYLVANIA

To Mowgli.

Author's Note

This is the sixth published novel in the *Shannon* series. These six novels deal with different periods of Clay Shannon's life. Those who have not previously read a Shannon novel may wish to read the series in chronological order, rather than the order in which the books were published. The chronological order of Shannon's biography is as follows:

Shannon: Carrying the Star
Shannon: The Road to Whiskey Creek
Shannon's Law
Shannon's Way
Shannon: U.S. Marshal
Shannon's Ride

Readers of previously published Shannon novels will find that *Shannon: The Road to Whiskey Creek* covers the period in Shannon's life between his adven-

1

tures as a young lawman in Longhorn, Kansas, described in *Shannon: Carrying the Star,* and his arrival more than ten years later in Whiskey Creek, the setting for *Shannon's Law*, the volume that was published first.

PART ONE

TOP OF THE WORLD

Chapter One
The Marshal of Stanleyville

Clay Shannon stood on the boardwalk, watching the end of an era. The small herd of cattle plodding along the main street of the town looked tired and dispirited, and the half-dozen riders escorting them were dusty and obviously discontented.

"Sad, isn't it?" said a voice. Shannon turned and found the mayor of Stanleyville, Kansas, standing beside him. The president of the bank was with him, and neither man looked very happy.

"A year ago this time we had thousands of animals coming through here each month," the mayor said. "This year it's been just a few small herds, and they tell me this sorry-looking bunch is the last one we'll have this season."

"It may be the last one we'll ever have," the banker

said, eyeing the passing animals disconsolately. "Now that the railroad's gone through south of here, the big Texas outfits aren't going to be coming this way anymore."

"Times change," Shannon said. "Towns have to change with them."

"You've seen it often enough to know," the mayor grumbled. "It's happening in all the Kansas trail towns. Boom and then bust when the trail herds stop coming. I guess it's our turn now."

He shook his head.

"Oh, well," he added, "maybe it won't be so bad. The homesteaders are moving into the region—they'll bring in enough business to keep Stanleyville going for awhile."

"Sodbusters don't have any money," said the banker sourly. "And if they borrow it, they go broke and can't pay it back."

"Nothing wrong with farmers," Shannon said. "They won't make as much trouble for the town as the trail herders have. Maybe things will be a bit more peaceful around here."

"If it gets too peaceful," the banker said meaningfully, "we won't need a marshal anymore."

Shannon laughed.

"Won't be the first time I've been fired," he said. "And there's always another town somewhere that isn't so peaceful."

"Hello," said the mayor. "What's this?"

A small man dressed in eastern clothes had come hurrying along the boardwalk and was pushing his way past the mayor and the banker.

"Marshal Shannon?" he asked eagerly, holding out his hand. "Marshal Clay Shannon?"

Shannon ignored the outstretched hand.

"I'm Shannon," he acknowledged. "What can I do for you?"

"Peabody's the name," the small man said. "Josiah Peabody. I'm a reporter for the *St. Louis World-Tribune*. Maybe you've read some of my stuff."

"No," Shannon said, "I'm afraid not. What can I do for you, Mr. Peabody?"

"I've come all the way to Stanleyville to write a story for my paper about you, Mr. Shannon. Do you have a few minutes?"

Shannon's brow furrowed.

"A story?" he said. "Why would you want to do that?"

"Oh, your name is well-known in Missouri, Mr. Shannon," Peabody said breathlessly. "You've got a reputation, you have. You've been a lawman in some of the toughest cow towns in Kansas—Wichita, Abilene, Ellsworth, Caldwell, Longhorn, even Dodge. Fastest gun on the frontier, they say. Why, I hear you've killed dozens of outlaws—all in fair fights, of course."

Shannon stared at him in astonishment.

"I think you've got the wrong man," he said uncomfortably.

"Oh, no," Peabody burbled. "Our readers would love to read about you, Marshal. Why, you're famous."

Shannon frowned.

"Look, Mister, er, Peabody," he said, "I don't want to be rude, but I'm really not interested in being interviewed for some newspaper. Besides, I haven't killed dozens of men and I'm certainly not the fastest gun on the frontier."

"I'm not so sure about that," the mayor said, laughing. "I've seen you draw." He reached out and shook hands with the reporter.

"I'm John Carswell, Mr. Peabody," he said. "I'm the mayor of Stanleyville. I'll be glad to talk with you. I can tell you a few tales about Marshal Shannon here that your readers would really enjoy. Let's go over to my office and I'll give you a good story. My name is spelled C-A-R-S-W-E-L-L, in case you want to include it in your article."

Peabody looked pained. Clearly he was not interested in writing about local politicians.

"Well," he said lamely, "perhaps Marshal Shannon could come with us. Would you do that, Marshal?"

Shannon did not answer. He was watching one of the riders at the rear of the passing cattle herd. A sudden gust of wind had kicked up a dust devil in front of the cowhand's roan horse and had spooked the animal. It reared up, causing the man to slip from the saddle and fall heavily to the ground. Screaming curses, the cowpuncher leaped up and began jerking savagely at the horse's reins. This further frightened the mustang, which again reared up and then tried to back away from the shouting man, starting to drag him along the street. Infuriated, the man drew his six-gun and slammed it against the side of the horse's head. Stunned, the horse sank to its knees. The man raised the pistol and delivered another blow to the horse's bowed head, still bellowing obscenities at the poor animal.

"Excuse me, gentlemen," Shannon said. "I'll be right back."

He stepped off the boardwalk and strode across the dusty street. The enraged cowhand saw him approaching and turned to face him, his six-gun still in hand.

"Whadda *you* want?" he snarled.

"I'd like to buy your horse," Shannon said, smiling pleasantly.

"What?" the man said, taken aback.

"I said, I'd like to buy your horse," Shannon replied. "I'll give you twenty dollars for him." He reached into his pocket, produced a twenty-dollar gold piece, and held it out. The cowpuncher stared at the coin, confused by this unexpected turn of events.

"What am I gonna do without a horse?" he demanded.

"Your trail drive's over. You don't need a horse," Shannon said, still smiling. He held the gleaming coin directly in front of the man's face. "Twenty dollars.

With that much in your pocket, you can take the stage-coach and ride in style back to Texas. What about it?"

"I dunno," said the cowboy, still somewhat muddled. For a man whose monthly pay was only fifteen dollars, this was a handsome offer.

"Well, if you're not interested . . ." Shannon said, starting to put the gold piece back into his pocket.

"Wait a minute," the man said, holstering his revolver. "What about my saddle and bridle?"

"You keep the saddle," Shannon said. "The bridle goes with the horse."

"Okay," the man said grudgingly, reaching for the coin. "It's a deal."

Shannon handed him the money and took the reins. As the cowboy unsaddled, Shannon examined the animal, noting the scars along its sides.

"I'll buy your spurs, too," Shannon said, indicating the sharp-roweled spurs on the cowhand's boots. "Five dollars."

The man looked at him suspiciously for a moment, then shrugged and bent to undo the spurs. Shannon took them and handed over another coin. The cow-puncher shouldered the saddle and started to walk after the departing cattle.

"I'll also take your gun," Shannon said.

"You wanna buy my gun?" the cowpuncher cried, startled.

"Not *buy*," Shannon said. *"Take."* He touched the

star on his shirt. "Town ordinance. You can pick it up at the marshal's office when your outfit leaves town."

The man dropped the saddle and squared off, his hand hovering above his holster.

"No two-bit Kansas tin star is takin' my gun," he said belligerently.

Shannon shook his head. It was not the first time he had heard those words from a Texas cowhand.

"Play it smart, cowboy," he said. "You've got twenty-five extra dollars in your pocket and your whole life ahead of you. Just hand over the hardware and go on your way while you still can."

"Better do as he says, Peck," said someone to Shannon's left. "This is one lawman you don't want to fool with."

Shannon recognized the voice immediately.

"Hello, Kip," Shannon said without turning. "Didn't know you were ramrodding this outfit."

The Texas ranch foreman swung down out of the saddle and stood beside him.

"Took over a couple of months ago. Haven't seen you since Dodge City, Clay. How've you been?"

"Doing fine," Shannon said, still watching the irate cowpuncher. "I take it this character is one of yours?"

"Yeah," said the foreman. "Worse luck. Go on, Peck, give him the gunbelt, then make tracks for the railroad corral. One of the boys will give you a ride back to camp."

Glaring at Shannon, the cowhand handed over the gunbelt.

"One other little thing," Shannon said quietly.

"Now what?" the man mumbled.

"If I ever see you treating a horse that way again," Shannon said, *"I'll kill you."*

The cowhand gaped at him, then turned beet red. He started to reach for his side, then remembered that he had already turned his gunbelt over to the marshal.

"I'll see you again, lawman," he growled.

"Not if you're lucky," Shannon replied.

The cowhand glared at him and stomped off.

The Texas foreman laughed.

"You haven't changed a bit," he said to Shannon. "Or maybe you have. You gave that saddle bum more than a month's pay for a horse you don't want and don't need. A few years ago, you'd have just slapped him alongside the head with that fancy six-gun of yours and tossed him in jail."

"Getting mellow with age, I guess," Shannon said. He hesitated, trying to think what he should do with the horse. Then he looked toward the boardwalk, where a large crowd had gathered to watch his encounter with the cowpuncher. The teenaged son of the widow who ran the general store was standing among the spectators.

"Jimmy," he said, "come here a minute, will you?"

The boy hurried over, looking apprehensively at Shannon.

"I hear your mother's cart horse died," he said.

"Yes, sir," the boy replied. "Makes it hard for us, because now we can't use the cart to make deliveries, and Ma says we can't afford to buy another."

"Here," Shannon said, handing him the roan horse's reins. "Give this old fellow to your mother with my compliments. Tell her to be good to him—he's earned a little kindness."

The boy beamed.

"Gosh," he said. "Thanks, Marshal."

He took the reins and hurried away.

Shannon walked back to the boardwalk, where he introduced the Texas foreman to the mayor and the banker.

"Gentlemen," he said, "this is Kip Howard, the ramrod of that outfit that just came through. He's trailed more cattle into Kansas than any man alive."

They shook hands, and talked for a few moments about cattle and cattle drives. Then Howard turned to Shannon.

"I've got to catch up with the herd," he said, "if you can call that a herd. Good to see you again, Clay."

He mounted his horse, waved, and rode away.

The reporter, Peabody, was still hovering nearby.

"That was really something to see, Marshal," he squeaked. "You did all that just for an old broken-down horse! It's amazing!"

Shannon shrugged.

"Don't make too much out of it, Mr. Peabody," he

said. "If you were the one being beaten, I'd probably have done the same for you."

"What about my story, Mr. Shannon?" the reporter said. "I still want to hear about some of your gunfights."

Shannon sighed.

"I wouldn't make very interesting reading," he said. "Tell you what, though, if you're interested in fast guns, I may be able to help you. You ever hear of a lawman named Cash Bonham?"

"No," said the reporter slowly. "Never. You mean he's faster on the draw than you?"

"Much faster. Killed more than a hundred men, I'm told. Maybe two or three hundred. Your readers would love him. Look, it's past my dinnertime. Come on down to the restaurant with me and I'll tell you about Cash while I eat."

He departed with the reporter hurrying along beside him, scribbling notes on a pad that he had taken from his pocket.

"Well, now I've seen everything," the banker said, watching them go. "First Shannon nearly gets himself killed over a wind-broke horse, and now he's telling that nitwit reporter a lot of tall tales just to shut him up."

"They're tall tales, all right," the mayor said. "I know Cash Bonham. Met him in Kansas City last year. He and Shannon were deputy town marshals together in Longhorn. Bonham told me that the only time he ever matched draws with Shannon, Shannon beat him by a country mile."

Chapter Two
Falling

The ticking of the clock on the office wall was the only sound breaking the stillness of the hot afternoon. Shannon sat at his desk, idly thumbing through some old wanted posters. He paused, looking reflectively at one of them. The face was familiar. He scowled, trying to remember.

That gunfight in Cottonwood last year, Shannon thought. *He shot another deputy, and I shot him. Good riddance.* He tossed the poster into the wastebasket by his desk, and continued through the pile.

A trickle of sweat coursed down his cheek; he pushed the posters aside and walked to the door of the office to get some air. The street was empty, the hardened dirt baking silently in the sun. The only living thing in sight was a farmer loading some barbed wire onto a wagon in front of the general store.

Then Shannon heard footsteps on the boardwalk and turned to find Stanleyville's mayor bearing down on him.

"Afternoon, Clay," the mayor said. "Hot enough for you?"

Shannon smiled tolerantly. Mayor Carswell's speech tended to be filled with such clichés. Shannon supposed it was a function of political life, like kissing babies.

"Quiet enough, at any rate," Shannon said.

The mayor glanced at the silent street and grimaced.

"Yeah, much too quiet. One sodbuster at the store, and that's it. I saw a couple of stray dogs awhile ago, but stray dogs don't spend money. If this keeps up, half the businesses in town will be broke by fall. Almost makes you wish the trail herds were still coming."

"Almost," Shannon said.

"Heard you made an arrest yesterday," said the mayor.

"Not much of one. It was Pete, drunk as usual, lying asleep in the sun. Had to toss him in a cell to keep him from getting heatstroke."

"Sounds like your trade is as slow as everybody else's," said the mayor.

"I don't mind," Shannon said. "At least it's restful."

"That's the trouble. There's no more action here. No more people crowding into town to shop, socialize, or just carouse in the saloons. No more hustle and bustle, not even on the weekends. This town is dying of terminal boredom, my friend."

A lone horseman appeared, riding slowly down the main street toward them.

"Perhaps that's a customer coming now," Shannon said encouragingly.

"I'll believe it when I see him spending money," the mayor snorted. "Well, I'm on the way home for lunch. Maybe my wife will have some exciting tales to tell about her sewing circle meeting this morning."

He went on his way, pausing only to wipe the perspiration from the sweatband of his hat.

Shannon was watching the approaching rider with increasing interest. The man was tall, spare, and dressed in black. Shannon's experienced eye detected the tied-down holster beneath his coat.

Gunfighter, Shannon thought. *Maybe we're in for a little excitement after all.*

From beneath the shadow cast by the brim of his hat, the rider was looking around at the signs hanging from the storefronts. Suddenly he turned his mount and rode up to the hitchrail in front of Shannon's office. As he swung down off the horse, Shannon at last saw his face clearly.

"Hello, Cash," he said, laughing. "What brings you to the booming city of Stanleyville?"

Cash Bonham stepped up onto the boardwalk and shook his hand.

"Hello, Clay," he said. "Heard you were the law here. How's business?"

"There isn't any," Shannon said, gesturing at the empty street. "Come on inside where we can talk out of the sun."

When they were seated in Shannon's office, Shannon glanced at Bonham's vest. There were pinholes in the cloth, but no badge was visible.

"Don't see any star," Shannon said. "You give up packing one?"

"Not on purpose," Bonham said. "I was marshaling up in Monkton, but things got so quiet I was invited to look elsewhere for employment. On my way now to a job further south. Cattle country, little town, doesn't sound like much, but at least it pays eating money."

"I'm glad you decided to come through here. It's nice to see you again."

"Well, I wanted to stop by because I've got a bone to pick with you. Why did you send that infernal reporter after me? Biggest pest I ever saw. Wanted to write my life story for some rag back in St. Louis."

"Sorry," Shannon said. "I had to get rid of him, and I thought you might enjoy being famous."

"Not me. I sent him chasing off after Slick Carter—told him Slick was the man to write about."

"Who's Slick Carter?" Shannon said.

"No idea," Bonham replied with a grin. "I made him up just to get rid of the newspaper guy. Told him there was a lightning-fast gunfighter named Slick Carter down in Fort James who had killed five hundred men, and our literary friend headed off in that direction, practically salivating to interview the great man."

Shannon stood up and lifted his hat from a peg by the door.

"Let's go over to the saloon," he said. "The beer's warm, but at least it's wet, and it might cut some of that dust you've been breathing on the trail."

They were the only ones in the saloon, so there was no difficulty finding a table.

"You're right," Bonham said, taking a pull at the mug the sleepy bartender had brought over. "It's warm. Say, I just missed seeing you in Cottonwood—I came through shortly after you'd left."

"The town was getting tame," Shannon said. "This one was still wide open, and they sent for me to handle the trial herders. Now look at it. Hard to believe that it was once just as wild as Longhorn, isn't it?"

"It's happening all over, Clay. No more trail herds, no more cowhands, civilization breaking out everywhere."

"You sound like our mayor."

"Your mayor's right. It's only noon in Stanleyville, Clay, but it's nearly sundown in the West for men like you and me. We've been riding high for years, cocks of the walk, fast guns and big reputations. But the country's changing. New people, new ways. We're dinosaurs, Clay. The big towns don't need us anymore. Pretty soon the small ones won't either. We're falling, Clay, and it's a long way down."

"Take it easy, Cash," Shannon said. "Things aren't all that bad."

"Not for you, maybe, not yet anyway. You're on top of the world here, Clay. Nice office, good salary, respected citizen. Even got journalists trailing after you. But enjoy it while you can, my friend. The twilight is coming for all of us who carry the star."

They talked for a while, and then Shannon took Bonham over to the café for some lunch. As they ate, he urged Bonham to stay overnight, but Bonham declined.

"Got to get going," he said. "Glad we could spend some time together, though. Those were good days in Longhorn. Too bad they're just a memory."

He rode away down the sunbaked street, and disappeared into the haze.

Shannon stood at the edge of the boardwalk, watching him go. Bonham's gloomy predictions troubled him. Thoughtfully, he looked around him, seeing again the quiet, dusty emptiness of the street. Even the lone farmer had left. Stanleyville lay slumbering in the afternoon sun.

I wonder, Shannon thought. *Could Cash be right?*

The days passed, each one dawning as hot as the ones before it. One morning, Shannon came to the office early, hoping to get some paperwork done before the heat became too oppressive. He was still at work when, shortly before noon, a shadow filled the open office doorway. Shannon looked up and saw Mayor Carswell standing there, a peculiar expression on his face.

"Got a minute, Clay?" he asked hesitantly.

Shannon put down his pen and leaned back in his chair.

"Certainly, Mayor," he replied. "Have a seat. What can I do for you?"

Carswell walked into the office but remained standing in front of Shannon's desk. Shannon found this disquieting. It was not like the mayor to be so diffident.

"City Council meeting just broke up," Carswell said. "I've got something to tell you."

Shannon sensed immediately what was coming.

"We, uh, we've got to let you go, Marshal," the mayor continued. "I'm sorry. We talked about it for a long time at the meeting. Now that the cattle drives don't come anymore, the town's going broke. We just don't have the money to pay you and your deputies now."

Shannon rubbed his eyes, waiting for the rest of it.

"I really feel bad about this," the mayor said, nervously twisting his hat in his hands. "We owe you a lot, Clay. You came here and risked your life a hundred times to make Stanleyville safe for the rest of us. But now things are quiet, and with no money coming into the town, we just can't afford a big police force anymore."

So, Shannon thought, *Cash was right. Twilight for the dinosaurs.*

"You're letting my deputies go, too?" he asked. "They both have families, you know."

"I know. I wish there was some other way."

"Who'll look after the town?" Shannon said. "You'll still need somebody."

"Old Man Thompson can take care of things," the mayor replied.

"He's seventy years old," Shannon said, "and the only thing he knows about law enforcement is how to sweep out the jail."

"I know," the mayor mumbled, "but we don't have to pay him, you see. At his age, all he wants is just room and board."

Shannon started to protest, but it was plain that there was no point in further discussion.

"All right, Mayor," he said. "And this is effective when?"

"Uh, well, immediately, I guess. Wish I could give you more time. I'm sure you'll find another job, though. You're young, and there are still plenty of places that need a good marshal."

"Oh, yes," Shannon said. "Plenty."

He unpinned the star from his shirt and placed it on the desktop.

"I'll move my personal things out of the office today," he said. "Anything else?"

"No, I guess not. Thanks, Clay. Thanks for under-standing."

The mayor opened his mouth to say something else, but stopped abruptly as gunshots echoed in the street.

"What the devil . . . ?" he cried.

Shannon hurried past him to the open door. The saloon keeper, Bill Ferris, was running across the street toward the office.

"Afternoon, Councilman," Shannon said laconically. "What's the problem?"

"Some drifter came into the saloon earlier, been drinking pretty heavy ever since. Went through a whole bottle of whiskey, then started on another, and now he's gone plumb crazy. Began shooting at the bottles behind the bar, and when my bartender, Sam, tried to interfere, he shot Sam too."

"Get out of my way," Shannon said, pushing past him. He strode across the street, pulling his ivory-handled Colt revolver from its holster as he went. He checked the cylinder of the Colt, then reholstered the weapon. Moving carefully along the front of the saloon, he peered through the window into the dark interior. There was another shot, and a female voice cried out in terror.

"Sounds like he's got Florence," Ferris said, coming up behind Shannon. "I hope he hasn't killed her. She's the only girl left—the others quit because business was so bad."

Shannon shoved him away and stepped through the swinging doors into the saloon. A large, bearded man in dirty clothing and a battered ten-gallon hat was standing in the middle of the floor with a six-gun in one big hand, holding the terrified saloon girl with the other. He turned to face Shannon, almost losing his balance in the process.

"Whadda you want?" he demanded, bleary-eyed, waving the revolver.

"Where's the bartender?" Shannon asked calmly.

"I'm back here, Marshal," said a voice from behind the bar. "He put a bullet in my arm. I'm bleeding bad."

"Let the girl go," Shannon said to the drunk.

Dazedly, the man loosened his grip on the frightened woman, and she ran past Shannon out the swinging doors, sobbing.

"Now drop the gun," Shannon said.

The drunken man stared at him in surprise.

"Nobody tells me to drop no gun," he shouted angrily, shaking the revolver at Shannon.

Shannon walked up to him, watching his eyes all the while. It was apparent that the man was so drunk that he was having difficulty even seeing Shannon, much less understanding what his approach meant.

"Whatcha think you're doin'?" he mumbled. "Don't come no closer or I'll . . ."

Shannon drew the Colt and smashed it against the man's temple. He collapsed in a heap at Shannon's feet, moaning. Shannon holstered the six-gun, then reached down and tossed the drunk's revolver over the bar. Grasping the fallen man by the back of his shirt,

Shannon dragged him across the floor of the saloon and out the door onto the boardwalk.

A small crowd had gathered around Ferris and the mayor, who had followed Shannon across to the saloon.

"Somebody get the doctor," Shannon said. "Sam's hurt."

He released his hold on the semiconscious drunk's shirt, letting him fall heavily to the boardwalk. The man moaned but made no attempt to get up. Shannon elbowed his way through the crowd and started across the street.

"Hey, wait," the mayor called. "What about this guy? Aren't you going to put him in jail?"

"Better get Old Man Thompson to do that," Shannon said. "I don't work here anymore."

PART TWO

CAULDRON COUNTY

Chapter Three
The Visitor

Shannon was in his room at the boarding house, packing his things. He had no idea where he was going to go, but he wanted to put Stanleyville behind him as soon as possible.

The knock on the door startled him. He slipped his six-gun out of its holster and moved to the wall beside the door.

"Who is it?" he called.

"Name's Curt Henderson," said a deep voice. "I'd like to talk to you if you can spare the time."

"Time's one thing I have plenty of right now," Shannon said.

He unlocked the door and opened it with his left hand, still holding his six-gun ready. The man standing in the corridor was tall, middle-aged, and well dressed.

He appeared to be unarmed, and his eyes met Shannon's with just a glint of humor in them. Shannon holstered the Colt.

"Come in, Mr. Henderson," he said. "Have a seat. What can I do for you?"

Henderson sat down on the room's one and only chair and folded his arms, waiting until Shannon had seated himself on the bed.

"I saw that little episode at the saloon today," he said. "That was nicely done."

"The man was too drunk to be much of a threat to anyone except saloon girls and unarmed bartenders," Shannon replied. "Was that what you wanted to talk about?"

"No, sir," Henderson chuckled. "I've just arrived in Stanleyville, Mr. Shannon. Came in on today's stage, and the fact is that I came looking for you."

"Looking for me?" Shannon asked, his hand instinctively moving nearer his holster. Henderson saw the movement and laughed again.

"Relax, son," he said. "I came to offer you a job."

Shannon blinked.

"Well, your timing's impeccable," he said. "As it happens, I find myself available at the moment."

"So I hear. Hard luck for you, but very fortunate for me."

"Perhaps you'd better explain."

"Of course," said Henderson. "Are you familiar with Cauldron County?"

"I've heard talk. Are you by any chance the Henderson who owns the Diamond Seven ranch down there?"

"The same. There's big trouble in Cauldron County, Mr. Shannon. We're on the verge of an all-out range war, and we need some help."

"What kind of help?" Shannon asked, his eyes narrowing. "I'm not a gunman for hire, Mr. Henderson, if that's what you're looking for."

"On the contrary," Henderson said. "I want you to take over as county sheriff and reestablish law and order in the county before things really get out of control."

"Don't you already have a sheriff down there?"

"We did. Bushwhacked outside of town a week ago."

"Dead?"

"Not quite. He'll pull through, but he's finished as a lawman. I want to appoint you to fill out his unexpired term."

Shannon found himself a bit nonplussed by this sudden development. When he got up that morning he was marshal of Stanleyville, by noon he was unemployed, and now, with the sun still high in the afternoon sky, he was being offered a star by one of the richest men in the territory.

Well, Cash, maybe we haven't fallen quite so far after all, Shannon thought.

But Henderson was looking at him in a strange way, as if there was something else he wanted to say but was reluctant to say it.

"What is it?" Shannon asked.

"The lawman that got drygulched," Henderson said. "He was a friend of yours."

Shannon's stomach knotted.

"Who was it?" he whispered.

Henderson reached into his coat and pulled out a newspaper clipping, which he handed to Shannon. "From our local paper," Henderson said.

Shannon read it with growing dismay.

We regret to report that last night our new county sheriff, Cash Bonham, was shot from an ambush just a mile outside of town. Sheriff Bonham survived the attack, but we are reliably informed that the bullet struck him in the back, damaging his spinal cord and leaving him paralyzed from the waist down. The identity of the perpetrators of this heinous crime is as yet unknown. It is to be hoped that a new sheriff will be appointed without delay to track them down.

Stunned, Shannon handed the clipping back to Henderson.

"I just saw Cash a few weeks ago," he said. "He told me he was on his way to a new job, but he didn't say where it was."

He got up and walked to the window. Pulling up the shade, he stared out into the sunlit street, still dazed by what he had just read.

"And now he's paralyzed?"

"Yes, I'm afraid it's true. You and Bonham are good friends, I take it?"

"Yes, we're good friends," Shannon said slowly. "But not the way you mean it, not friends in the sense that most people use the word. Lawmen sometimes develop a peculiar sort of professional bond, one that grows out of the nature of our business."

He paused, struggling to find the right words.

"You see," he continued, "when you carry a star, you have to depend upon the men you work with. You have to trust your life to them, and you know that they trust their lives to you. Because it's literally a matter of life and death, you learn very quickly who deserves that kind of trust and who doesn't. Cash was a man to be trusted."

"He spoke very highly of you," Henderson said. "He told me that you saved his life a couple of times when you were lawmen together back in Longhorn."

"Yes, and he saved mine, more than a couple of times. Is there any chance he'll ever walk again?"

"The doctor said there's always a chance, but it doesn't look too good right now. I'm sorry."

Shannon was still gazing blankly out the window, trying to bring some order to his jumbled thoughts.

"And you want me to take over for Cash?" he said at last. "Why me?"

"I asked Cash who we might get to replace him. He said we needed a man like you. In fact, what he said about you was very similar to what you just said about him. He said we could put our trust in you."

Shannon was still at the window, scenes of the past flashing through his mind. He and Cash facing down four drunken gunmen in the Longhorn schoolhouse. The two of them ducking stampeding cattle together in the alley outside the Yellow Dog Saloon. Cash covering his back in a dozen gunfights when the presence of a lesser man might have cost Shannon his life. And now, the worst image of all, Cash Bonham lying in a bed somewhere, crippled and in pain, his life as a lawman ended, perhaps forever.

"Well, what about it, Mr. Shannon?" Henderson was saying. "Will you take the job?"

"Yes," Shannon said. "I'll take the job."

"You haven't asked about the pay," Henderson reminded him.

"It doesn't matter," Shannon said bleakly. "I'll take the job."

As the sun sank in the west, Henderson related to Shannon the situation in Cauldron County.

"A year ago," he began, "Cauldron County was as good a place to call home as anywhere in the West. Nice country, nice people. There are two large ranches in the county—mine and Arch Cromwell's—but there are several smaller ranchers who are our neighbors, and for a long time we all got along very well. Cromwell and I never had any problems, and neither did our ranch hands. We shared the open range, shared the water, everybody minded his own business, and things were fine. The county seat, Cauldron City, was a quiet and prosperous town, the kind of place you'd be proud to live in."

"And then?"

Henderson's face darkened.

"And then," he said, "Arch Cromwell changed. He used to be friendly, open-minded, easy to deal with. Over a period of just a few months, he turned into a different person entirely—hostile, suspicious, belligerent, grasping."

"No apparent reason? A quarrel of some kind between you, perhaps?"

"No, no reason at all that I could see. Gradually he became aloof, then openly hostile. And that's when the troubles began."

"Such as?"

"First I started losing cattle—just a few at the beginning, but then more and more. Next, a rancher named Tom Lipton who owned a small spread next to mine was found dead one day, pinned under his horse at the bottom of a gulch. Everybody figured it was an accident—horse lost its footing, rolled down the slope on top of Tom, they said. No reason to suppose otherwise—not then, at least. Cromwell bought out Kate Lipton, Tom's niece, cheap. She couldn't keep the place going by herself, so she sold out and moved into town."

"Didn't Lipton have any hands working for him who could run the place for her?"

"Sure, but for some strange reason they all up and quit when Cromwell started negotiating with Lipton's niece to buy her out. Then, as soon as Cromwell had the deed to the Lipton place, he started moving cattle onto it—cattle with brands that look like they just might have been altered with a running iron. Meanwhile, more and more of Cromwell's old hands were leaving him. His people used to be good folks, so I hired some of them. When I asked them what was going on, they said things were getting pretty ugly at Cromwell's ranch. They told me that Cromwell was becoming meaner and meaner, having temper fits, yelling at his people and firing them for no reason. I heard he even horsewhipped one of his stable workers because the man didn't bring Cromwell's buggy up to the house fast enough when Cromwell told him to."

"It does sound pretty disagreeable," Shannon said.

"It gets worse," Henderson replied. "When he got shorthanded, Cromwell began to replace the old bunch with men of a different breed, a lot of hard-faced waddies with guns tied down, ramrodded by a man named Wade Stitch who looked like he'd be more at home in Yuma Territorial Prison than in Cauldron County."

Henderson had begun to pace the floor, and his voice grew harder as he continued.

"Once Stitch and his gunslingers appeared, funny things started happening in town. The owner of the saloon got killed during a brawl one Saturday night. Accidental shooting, the witnesses claimed—but the witnesses were all Cromwell's men. Cromwell took over the saloon, and after Bonham was shot, Cromwell moved in gambling equipment. Gambling's illegal in Cauldron County, but he just ignored the law, and before long he had a roaring business in the saloon. After that, the owner of the general store disappeared, just vanished one night, him and his wife both. Closed up the store one night and were gone the next morning without a word to anybody. Next thing we know, Cromwell's operating the store—got a piece of paper he claims is a bill of sale for the place from the former owners. Puts his own man in there to run the place, and suddenly the prices go sky high. Townsfolk were pretty unhappy about it, but it's the only store in town, so everybody has to pay."

"No other stores in the county?"

"Used to be one over by the county line. It burned down one night last month. Some of our townspeople tried sending wagons over to the next county to get supplies, but the wagons got held up, a couple of drivers were killed, and that was the end of that."

Shannon had been listening to all of this with growing puzzlement.

"Surely, Mr. Henderson, you could have stepped in sooner and stopped Cromwell yourself," he said. "You're a rich and powerful man. You must have plenty of men in your employ—enough to take on Cromwell."

"I have cowhands, Mr. Shannon. Not gunhands. They'd be no match for the kind of people Cromwell has brought in. And, in any case, the last thing I want is to start a full-fledged war in the county. I want Cromwell stopped, but I want it done legally and without violence, if that's possible. A bloody range war would set the county back twenty years, and I don't want to be responsible for that. We need law and order in Cauldron County, Mr. Shannon, not gunsmoke and anarchy. That's why I hired Cash. That's why I need you."

"What about your local law? Wasn't your county sheriff doing anything about all this—the one before Cash?"

"Not much. He was an elderly man who had been in office for many years. He resigned suddenly about two months ago and left town. I figure Cromwell paid him off or scared him out, one or the other. Nobody else in the county wanted the job—didn't want to tangle with Cromwell, apparently—so I had no choice but to look outside the county for a lawman. I'd known Cash from the days when he was marshaling in Wichita; sent for him and appointed him to serve the old sheriff's unexpired term. When Cash came in, he tried his best to get to the bottom of it all, but we weren't able to come up with any proof that Cromwell had done anything illegal."

"Did Cromwell try to run Cash out of the county?"

"Oh, yes. The same way he got rid of the old sheriff—bribes and threats."

"That wouldn't work with a man like Cash."

"Not a bit. Cash just kept going, trying to get the goods on Cromwell. He had a couple of run-ins with Cromwell's people in town. Had to shoot one of them, in fact. Finally, one day Cash decided to ride out to Cromwell's ranch to question him in person. He never made it back to town. The next morning somebody found him lying by the roadside with a hole in his back and brought him in. Our town doctor said that with that kind of a wound, most people would have died out there during the night. I guess Cash is lucky to be alive."

"If you can call being paralyzed lucky," Shannon said bitterly.

"Anyway," Henderson said, "that's the situation, and a nasty one it is. You sure you still want the job?"

"When are you leaving to go back to Cauldron County?" Shannon asked.

"Noon stage tomorrow. Shall I buy you a ticket?"

"No," Shannon said. "I've got an old buckskin stallion that I'm kind of fond of. I'll let him bring me. I'll be in the saddle at dawn, Mr. Henderson, and I'll see you in Cauldron County in three days."

"Watch your back on the way in. The trail leads right past Cromwell's ranch. Somebody might decide to take a shot a you before you even get to town."

"If they do," Shannon said, "it'll be the last mistake they ever make."

Chapter Four
The Sheriff of Cauldron County

The country through which Shannon rode was brown and empty. As he approached Cauldron County, the flat plains that surrounded Stanleyville had given way to rougher, more broken country, and the wagon road that he was following began to wind through low hills and across dry riverbeds. Shannon gave the buckskin its head, devoting his attention to a study of the land around him, watchful for signs of trouble. His night camps were dry and uncomfortable, but he did not care to advertise his presence with a fire.

On the third day he found himself passing features that the rancher, Henderson, had told him would mark his arrival in Cauldron County. One of the landmarks was a solemn reminder of his purpose in coming—a large wooden gate set between two tall, ancient-looking posts topped by a heavy crossbar. Behind the gate, a trail wound away into the hills. No buildings were visible beyond the gate, but the weathered letters on the sign hanging beneath the steer skull attached to the crossbar said *Cromwell Ranch,* and a smaller sign nailed to one of the posts proclaimed in newly painted letters *Keep Out. Trespassers Will Be Shot.*

"Welcome to Cauldron County," Shannon said to the plodding horse. "Hope the rest of the folk here are a little more friendly."

He rode more alertly now, for he knew that somewhere between the entrance to the Cromwell Ranch and the town limits ahead of him, Cash Bonham had met the bullet that struck him down. It was easy to see how Bonham had been ambushed in that country, with its rocky hills and deep ravines. A hundred men could have been hiding there waiting, and Shannon felt tangible relief when at last the rooftops of the town came into view.

Henderson had instructed Shannon to meet him at his lawyer's office when he arrived in town and as Shannon rode along the main street he soon saw the sign *Jason Taylor, Attorney at Law,* hanging over the boardwalk. Shannon had telegraphed ahead to let both men know his expected date of arrival, and Henderson was there, waiting for Shannon. The rancher greeted him warmly and invited him into the inner office, where he introduced to Shannon to the lawyer and Ezekiel Webster, the editor of the town's newspaper.

Jason Taylor reminded Shannon of the attorney with whom Shannon had been studying law as a young man, before his father's murder changed the course of his life. The newspaper editor, Webster, was a thin elderly man who greeted Shannon with an analytical eye that suggested to Shannon he was being measured for some future headline in the town newspaper.

"Let's get you sworn in," Henderson suggested. "Then we can talk."

The ceremony was brief, and Henderson pinned the star on Shannon's shirt.

"Well, folks," he said, "Cauldron County has a sheriff again."

"Yes," said the editor gloomily. "Let's hope he has better luck than the last two."

"I'd like to see Cash Bonham," Shannon said. "Where can I find him?"

"Doctor Evans moved him over to the boardinghouse," Henderson replied. "I wanted to take him out to my ranch, but Doc said he didn't want him moved too far just yet. Another few days, perhaps. Ma Donaldson runs the boardinghouse, and she's looking after Cash. Doing a good job of it, from what I can tell."

The room in the boardinghouse was clean and well kept, but it had about it the unmistakable odor of illness that permeates all sick rooms, a smell that Shannon hated. Against one wall of the room stood a big brass bed. Cash Bonham lay in the bed, his face pale and drawn.

"Hello, Clay," he said as Shannon entered. "Sorry I can't get up, but I suppose you know all about that. I see by the star on your shirt that Henderson talked you into it."

"He said you recommended me," Shannon said. "Thanks."

"Don't thank me yet," said Bonham. "Before you're through, you may be sorry I got you into this."

"Maybe," Shannon said. "What are your plans?"

"My brother's coming to take me back to his place in Colorado. Be here in a few days. I guess I can still make myself useful on a ranch—somehow."

"You can make yourself useful now," Shannon said. "Tell me what's going on here, what you learned before they drygulched you."

They talked for over an hour, with Shannon doing most of the listening.

"What do you make of this Cromwell fellow?" Shannon asked.

"I think he's crazy," Bonham said. "Mad as a hatter. Be careful with him, Clay. He's as mean as a rattlesnake with a toothache, and just as unpredictable."

"It sounds as if he's bribed and bullied most of the people in the county into going along with him," Shannon said. "Who's on our side, Cash? Whom can I trust?"

"Henderson, for starters," Bonham said. "He's a good man—too good, I think. He believes in law and order, wants to play this by the rules. He doesn't understand yet the kind of men he's up against. The newspaper editor's on our side, but he's all talk and editorials. It's a wonder somebody hasn't plugged him by now. Also, you've got a deputy. Nephew of the old sheriff I replaced. Nice kid, tries hard, hasn't got a clue. Reminds me of you when you first rode into Longhorn, green as grass, wants to be a lawman more than anything. Try to keep him alive, will you?"

"Like you did me when I was that age," Shannon said with a gentle smile.

"Yeah," Bonham said gruffly. "Something like that." He fell silent, and presently Shannon saw that he had fallen into an exhausted sleep.

Henderson was waiting for him outside the room. A young man wearing a deputy's star was with him.

"Clay, this is Randy Cutler," Henderson said.

"I'm mighty glad to meet you, Mr. Shannon," Cutler said, pumping Shannon's hand enthusiastically. "I've heard a lot about you, sir, and it's a real honor to be your deputy."

"How's Cash doing?" Henderson asked.

"As well as you could expect," Shannon said. "Anything else happening that I should know about?"

"Got one piece of news today that doesn't sit very well," Henderson replied. "Cromwell's bullied the town council into appointing Wade Stitch town marshal. That's not going to make it any easier for us."

"We'll manage," Shannon said. "It won't be the first time I've gone up against a crooked lawman. Look, I left my horse at the livery stable. Where can I put my gear?"

"I want you to stay at our ranch," Henderson said. "My daughter Sarah's looking forward to meeting you."

Shannon shook his head.

"I've got to appear neutral if we're going to resolve all of this short of bloodshed," Shannon said. "If I'm at your ranch, I'm branded as your man, and I'll also be too far from the county seat to keep track of what's going on. I'll settle for a room here in Ma's boardinghouse."

"Whatever you want to do is fine with me," Henderson said. "Randy, could you find Ma and tell her she's got another guest, and then put Clay's things in his room?"

"Sure, Mr. Henderson," the deputy said. "Be right back, Mr. Shannon, in case you need me."

When Cutler had hurried away, Henderson spoke again to Shannon.

"I understand why you want to room in town," he said, "but at least come out to my place tonight. I'm having a little get-together of our neighbors. It's my daughter's birthday, and we're going to try to forget our troubles for a while and have a little fun. You can ride out with that young deputy of yours. He'll show you the way. He knows it well enough." He looked around to make sure that Randy Cutler was out of earshot, and then grinned at Shannon. "He's sweet on my daughter, and if I'm not mistaken, the feeling is mutual. Nothing like watching young love in bloom to keep us old folks entertained."

A commotion in the street outside the boardinghouse interrupted their conversation. Shannon and Henderson moved quickly out onto the front porch and saw a half-dozen men engaged in a brawl in the middle of the street. Four of the men were paired off, swinging at each other with their bare fists, while another two were wrestling in the dust. Curses, shouts, grunts, and occasional yelps of pain provided the background for the encounter.

Randy Cutler came running out of the boarding-house. He hurried past Shannon and Curt Henderson, calling to the men to stop fighting. They paid no attention to him, so Cutler, still shouting for them to stop, dived into the middle of the group and began to pull the combatants apart. Immediately the irate men turned on him, pummeling him. One of them knocked Cutler to the ground and drew back his boot to kick the fallen deputy in the ribs.

Shannon drew his Colt and fired one shot into the air. As if by magic, the brawlers froze in position, twisting their heads around in surprise.

"You with your foot in the air," Shannon said. "If you

want to keep it attached to your leg, lower it to the ground—slowly. The rest of you stand still. Randy, are you all right?"

The deputy scrambled to his feet, looking sheepish.

"Yessir," he said, retrieving his hat from the dirt.

"Mr. Henderson, do you know these men?" Shannon asked.

"Yeah," the rancher replied. Those three are my hands. The rest are Cromwell's."

"They jumped us, Mr. Henderson," said one of the Diamond Seven hands. "We wasn't doing nuthin'."

"They was blockin' the sidewalk, Henderson," said a Cromwell man. "All we wanted to do was get past."

"Excellent reasons for trying to beat each other's brains in," Shannon said, "but the fun's over now. You Cromwell men go on your way. Mr. Henderson, I'd be obliged if you'd ask your people to do the same."

"Go on back to the ranch, boys," Henderson said. "We'll talk about this later."

The two groups drifted away, casting smoldering looks back at each other.

"Mr. Henderson," Shannon said, "I'll see you at your ranch tonight. Thank you for inviting me. Meanwhile, perhaps Deputy Cutler will be kind enough to show me where the sheriff's office is."

The office was typical for its kind, a bare room with a jail attached at the rear. Shannon looked around, wondering why all such places looked so similar. It was as if they were all built to the same pattern, all uncomfortable and all depressing. *I've spent my life in places like this,* Shannon thought. *How sad.*

"Say, uh, thanks for stepping in back there," Randy Cutler said. "I guess I didn't handle that too well."

"That's an understatement," Shannon said. "Cash Bonham asked me to keep you alive. I can see that's going to be a real challenge."

"What did I do wrong?" Cutler asked forlornly.

"Everything," Shannon said. "In the first place, don't ever try to break up a brawl that large by yourself if you can avoid it. If no backup is available, let them fight it out until the odds are reduced a little. It was only a fistfight, so unless somebody drew a knife or gun, nobody was going to get killed. Second, you walked right into the middle of them, got yourself surrounded. If you have to wade in to stop it, work from the outside inward. Don't let anybody get behind you—keep the fight in front of you so you can see if somebody is going to draw on you. Third, if you have to get into the middle of something, make sure you protect your own six-gun while you're in there. You're lucky one of those people didn't grab it right out of your holster and beat you over the head with it, or shoot you on the spot. A lot of peace officers have been killed with their own weapons. Don't let it happen to you."

Cutler hung his head in embarrassment. Shannon had to struggle to keep from laughing; Cutler reminded him of a puppy who had just been scolded for soiling the carpet.

"One other thing," Shannon said. Cutler winced.

"Y-y-yes, sir?" he whispered.

"You did some things right too," Shannon said. "You showed plenty of guts going after them like that. And your instinct was to step in to stop the trouble before it got any worse—that's a reaction that I'd expect from any good lawman. The other things can be learned, but the courage and the instinct have to be there to start with. You'll be a good lawman, Randy, if you live long enough."

Cutler brightened perceptibly at this last statement, and Shannon chuckled at the boy's obvious gratitude.

"Here endeth the lesson," Shannon said. "Let's go get a cup of coffee."

Chapter Five
Friends and Enemies

The birthday party at the Diamond Seven was in full sway when Shannon and Randy Cutler arrived. They tied their horses to the already crowded hitchrail by the bunkhouse and walked across to the large yard in front of the main house where the guests had gathered. It was a pretty scene, Shannon thought, with colored paper lanterns strung across the porch and yard and the sound of the fiddlers playing a merry tune for the dancers swinging their partners in time to the music. Curt Henderson saw the two lawmen approaching and, after greeting them, led them over to a group of people standing on the house's long front verandah.

"Sheriff," Henderson said, "I'd like you to meet my daughter, Sarah, the birthday girl."

Shannon noted three things about Sarah Henderson

immediately. She was very young, she was very pretty, and all the time she was exchanging greetings with Shannon her gaze kept darting toward Randy Cutler, who was standing immediately beside Shannon. Clearly, Henderson's comment about a budding romance between Sarah and the deputy was entirely accurate.

"And this is my son, Todd," Henderson was saying.

Todd Henderson was older than Sarah, shorter than his father, but otherwise closely resembling him. His handshake was hearty.

"Dad's told me a lot of good things about you, Sheriff," the younger Henderson said. "We're glad you're here. I'm sorry about Mr. Bonham—I understand he's a friend of yours."

"Thank you," Shannon said. "I hope I can live up to your father's advanced billing."

Henderson turned and touched the arm of a young woman standing close behind him.

"This is Kate Lipton, Sheriff," he said. "She's the niece of Tom Lipton, the rancher who, er, died recently."

Shannon found himself looking into a pair of dark green eyes that were framed by auburn hair and accompanied by a smile that, Shannon decided, must have melted the heart of many a Cauldron County man.

"A pleasure," he mumbled, gazing into the depths of those remarkable eyes.

"Thank you for coming to our aid, Mr. Shannon," Kate Lipton said. "We're all very grateful to you."

"I'm afraid I haven't done anything yet," Shannon said. He plucked at his shirt collar, wondering why he suddenly felt so warm.

Shannon would have liked to stay and talk with Kate Lipton longer, but Curt Henderson insisted on taking him around the yard to introduce him to the other guests. Shannon smiled dutifully, shaking hands and struggling unsuccessfully to remember all of the names. Once he looked back at the house and was strangely pleased to see that Kate Lipton was still standing on the verandah, watching him.

"There they go," Curt Henderson was saying. "Told you they were sweet on each other."

Sarah Henderson and Randy Cutler were walking slowly, hand in hand, out of the circle of light cast by the lanterns, down toward the cottonwood trees that lined the nearby stream.

"Not sure I'd let my daughter go wandering off like that with anybody but Randy," Henderson mused. "But he's a nice kid, and I could do worse for a son-in-law. Take care of him, Clay."

"I'll try," Shannon said. "But he'd be a lot safer if he'd unpin that deputy's badge and take up cattle ranching."

"Sarah agrees with you," Henderson said, "but Randy's bound and determined to be a lawman."

"How does your wife feel about Sarah potentially marrying a deputy sheriff?" Shannon asked.

"My wife's dead, Clay. Four years ago. But she

always liked Randy when he was a kid, so perhaps she wouldn't mind too much. Say, what's this?"

A buggy was approaching the house, followed by two horsemen. The driver of the buggy pulled up at the end of the verandah, climbed out, and then helped his female passenger down as well. The two riders dismounted and stood waiting.

"Incredible!" Henderson gasped.

"What's incredible?" Shannon asked.

"That's Arch Cromwell!" Henderson said. "The woman's his sister, Marian. What in the devil do they think they're doing, coming here?"

"I take it they weren't invited?"

"Absolutely not. I can't believe Cromwell would have the nerve."

"Well, since he's here, perhaps you'll introduce me," Shannon suggested.

Arch Cromwell was tall and lean, almost cadaverous. His eyes were deep-set, with dark circles under them. They gleamed brightly as Henderson and Shannon approached.

"Good evening, Curt," Cromwell said cheerfully. "Seems like a nice party. Mind if my sister and I join the fun?"

"Looks like the fun's over," Henderson said. "You seem to have put a damper on it."

He gestured at the guests, who had ceased talking and dancing and were now standing around silently, watching. The music had stopped as well.

Todd Henderson was approaching rapidly looking very annoyed.

"What's Cromwell doing here, Dad?" Todd demanded. "Did you invite him?"

"No," Henderson said. "I did not. This is a private party, Arch. Why are you here?"

Cromwell laughed. It was not a good laugh, Shannon thought. There was an edge beneath it that made it a little disturbing.

"Like I said, Curt," Cromwell replied. "Just wanted to join the fun. After all, I am your neighbor, right?"

"You're not the kind of neighbor I'd like to have," Henderson said. "And there are a lot of people here tonight who feel the same way. You took a chance even coming here. There are a couple of widows in the crowd who'd like to ask you what happened to their husbands."

Todd stepped between his father and the Cromwells.

"This is my sister's birthday party, Cromwell," he said hotly, "and you're not welcome here. Take those two gunmen you brought along and go home before there's trouble."

"My, my, the cub growls just like his father," Cromwell laughed. "Come on, boy, lighten up."

"Dad, get rid of him, please," Todd said to his father. "Sarah doesn't want him here and neither do I."

The elder Henderson shook his head sadly.

"No, he can stay," the rancher said with reluctance. "Invited or not, he's a guest on my premises now, and I won't turn him away. Not this time, at least. All right Arch, you and your sister can join us. Marian, I'm sorry about this unfriendly greeting you've received. You're welcome here anytime, even though your brother is not."

"Thank you, Curt," she said. "I wish somehow you two could patch up your differences. We all used to be such good friends."

"That was a few dead men and a lot of rustled cattle ago," said Todd Henderson angrily.

"That's enough, Todd," Curt Henderson said. "Go find Sarah and Randy. I think they went down by the river."

Todd Henderson gave Cromwell one last glare and strode off.

"And this, I take it, is our new sheriff," Cromwell said, looking at Shannon. "Welcome to Cauldron County, Mr. Shannon. Curt, I'd like to talk with the sheriff alone for a moment, if I may."

Henderson hesitated, glancing at Shannon.

"It's all right," Shannon said. "I'll rejoin you in a few minutes."

Gradually, the conversation and dancing began again, but it was not as spirited as it had been, and Shannon noted the resentful looks being directed at Arch Cromwell.

"I want to get off on the right foot with you, Shannon," Cromwell began. "I'm sure you've heard a lot of bad things about me, and I'm glad to have a chance to set the record straight."

"Who shot Cash Bonham?" Shannon said, watching for Cromwell's reaction.

"You don't beat about the bush, do you?" Cromwell remarked with a tart smile. "Yes, it's a real shame about Bonham, but I have no idea who did it. Do you?"

"Not yet," Shannon said, "but I mean to find out."

Cromwell's face hardened, and his eyes grew mean.

"Look, Shannon," he said, "I'm a big man in this country now. I own a large ranch and I'm acquiring other land as well. I own the only general store in the county, and anybody that wants to buy anything buys it from me—at my prices. I've got men, money, cattle, power. I can make or break anyone I choose. In short, you'd do well to stay out of my way."

He laughed again, but the laugh was filled with malice, not humor.

"And don't count too much on Henderson backing you, if you plan to go up against me," he said. "Before I'm through, I may own the Diamond Seven too."

"I doubt that the Hendersons will allow that to happen," Shannon said.

"That could change," Cromwell sneered. "Everybody has their price. Besides, who knows, I might even get that pretty little Sarah to marry me. I wouldn't mind having her and the Diamond Seven too. What do you think of that?"

Before Shannon could answer, a female voice knifed out of the darkness.

"I think it's *disgusting,*" Sarah Henderson said. She

had come up behind Cromwell and had overheard the last part of the conversation. Randy Cutler was standing beside her, looking bewildered.

"You make me *sick,* Cromwell," Sarah cried. "I wouldn't marry you if—"

"What's going on?" Todd Henderson said, pushing past Sarah and looking from her to Cromwell.

"This—this pig says he wants to *marry* me!" Sarah said.

Todd Henderson grabbed Cromwell by the front of his shirt and pushed his face up against the older man's.

"Get off this property, Cromwell," he said, "and stay off. If I ever hear of you even speaking to my sister again, I'll kill you."

Cromwell's two ranch hands had left their positions by the buggy and were running toward them, reaching for their six-guns. Several of the Diamond Seven men had left their women and were approaching also. Shannon could see that things were about to get out of hand, and that he had to act quickly. Drawing his Colt, he stepped in between Cromwell and the approaching men.

"That's close enough, boys," he said, covering them. "And you Diamond Seven people, back off. I'll handle this."

Still watching Cromwell's men, Shannon turned his head slightly so that he could speak to Todd Henderson and Cromwell behind him.

"Todd, let go of Cromwell's shirt and move away from him. Randy, take Sarah into the house and stay with her until I get there. As for you, Cromwell, I think you've worn out whatever small welcome you had here, so I suggest that you take your sister and your men and leave now, before there's any more unpleasantness."

Cromwell's eyes now glistened with annoyance, and when he spoke his voice was harsh.

"You're making a mistake taking Henderson's side in this," he snarled. "A *big* mistake."

"I'm not taking anybody's side," Shannon said. "I'm here to enforce the law in this county. Anybody who breaks the law will answer to me, regardless of who it is."

"You're meddling in things you don't understand, Shannon," Cromwell rasped. "And don't give me that stuff about not being on anybody's side. You're Henderson's man, all right. He and his cronies gave you that tin star, but you won't have it long. There's an election next year, and I plan to run for sheriff myself."

"Why wait?" Shannon said. "Why not just bushwhack me like you did Cash Bonham?"

Cromwell's smile was poisonous.

"That's a thought, Shannon," he said. "Something for us *both* to keep in mind."

When the Cromwells and their men had gone, Henderson tried to revive the party, but his attempts to recapture the earlier gaiety were unsuccessful. As the guests began to drift away, Henderson took Shannon into the living room of the house. Sarah was sitting in a chair, her face stony, as Randy Cutler stood by her uncomfortably. Todd Henderson was there too, his expression like a thundercloud.

"I'm sorry, darlin'," Curt Henderson said to Sarah. "I'm afraid I've spoiled your birthday."

"Not you, Dad," Sarah Henderson said. "Cromwell. What a despicable piece of slime he is. The very thought of—"

"Sheriff," Todd Henderson interjected, "you've got to do something about Cromwell. Everybody knows about the crimes he's committed."

"I plan to do something about him, Todd," Shannon said quietly.

"Good," Todd snapped, "because if you don't, the rest of us will."

He stomped out of the room.

"Mr. Henderson," Shannon said, "we need to talk."

They went into Henderson's study and closed the door.

"Well, at least you've met Cromwell," Henderson said. "What do you think?"

"A very strange man," Shannon said. "He seems to change personalities as quickly as a chameleon changes its color."

"That's a good comparison, I guess," Henderson said. "So, now that you've met Cromwell and know the situation, what do we do?"

"I think the first thing to do is to break Cromwell's hold on the town. He's using that as his power base. Let's take it away from him."

"How?"

"One piece at a time. For starters, how would you like to own a general store?"

"You mean open one up in competition with Cromwell?"

"Exactly. Can you afford it?"

"Of course. There are several empty buildings in town, left by people who've gotten fed up and pulled out. We can get one of those and turn it into a store. I've got men and wagons to bring in the goods to stock it, but I'm no storekeeper. Somebody will have to run it."

"What about Miss Lipton? You said she'd moved into town, and she'll need an income now that her uncle's gone and Cromwell has her ranch."

Henderson nodded.

"Sounds good to me."

"Then let's ask her."

Henderson had detailed two of his men to escort Kate Lipton safely back to town. They were just about to leave when Henderson sent word asking her to join him in the study. As she entered, she looked questioningly at Henderson and Shannon.

Quickly, Shannon explained the proposal to her. She listened gravely, asked several questions, then nodded.

"I'll do it," she said. "And thank you—both of you."

"There, uh, there are still some details we need to work out," Shannon said hesitantly. "Perhaps when we get back to town, Miss Lipton and I could discuss them over dinner."

She paused, and the dark green eyes looked searchingly into Shannon's bright blue ones. Shannon wondered as he waited for her answer why his heart was beating so fast.

"I'd be delighted," she said. The smile she gave Shannon nearly stopped his heart completely.

Whoa, Shannon, he told himself. *You can't afford to get involved with someone now. You've got a job to do, and you need to concentrate on it if you want to live to see it through. You'd better keep your contacts with this lady strictly business.*

Then he looked again into Kate Lipton's green eyes, and realized with resignation that he would have a tough time taking his own advice.

Chapter Six
Confrontation

Two days later, Cash Bonham's brother arrived to take him home. Shannon went down to the boarding-house to see him off. When Shannon arrived, they had already placed Bonham in the covered wagon that would convey him to Colorado. Shannon climbed into the wagon and sat beside Bonham as he lay on the mattress that had been placed in the wagon beside to ease the passage over the rough roads. Although Bonham did not appear to be in any pain, it was evident he was deeply depressed.

"The doctor says that you may get better in time," Shannon offered. "He thinks the bullet may have only bruised the spinal cord. If so, you could be walking again in a matter of weeks."

"Maybe," Bonham said. "You and I both know it's

a long shot, but thanks for being cheerful about it, anyway."

"I'll write to you," Shannon said, "and let you know how things turn out here. Whoever put that slug in you is going to pay for it. I guarantee it."

Bonham reached over and shook Shannon's hand warmly.

"Be careful, Clay," Bonham said. "Don't underestimate Cromwell. He may be crazy, but he's as dangerous as a scorpion. And watch your back. I don't want to hear that you left Cauldron County the way I'm leaving it—or worse."

Shannon stood by, lost in thought, as the wagon moved off down the road, carrying Cash Bonham away to another life.

"That looks good," Curt Henderson said. He was standing in the street, watching as two of his men finished lifting a large sign into place on the building in front of them. The sign said *Henderson General Store,* and as the workers finished nailing it into place, Kate Lipton came out of the store and joined Shannon and Henderson.

"Have you got enough help in there, Kate?" Curt Henderson asked. "Stocking a store is a bit more of a job than I thought it would be."

"We're doing fine," Kate answered, smiling at Shannon. "Between Randy and Sarah and the men you sent with the wagons, we're about ready to open for business. We've set the prices as you told us to, Mr. Henderson. They're less than half of what Cromwell's store is charging. People will be able to buy the things they need again."

"Any reaction from Cromwell yet?" Shannon asked.

"Not a thing," Henderson replied. "A couple of his hands have been hanging around across the street there, watching what we're doing, but they haven't made any trouble that I can see."

"They will," Shannon said. "Cromwell isn't going to take this quietly."

"How's that apartment we fixed up for your above the store, Kate?" Henderson asked. "Not very fancy, but we'll try to make some improvements as we go along."

"It's fine," Kate Lipton said. "Sarah helped me decorate it. It'll do nicely."

"Then I guess we're about set," Henderson said. "Come on inside, Clay. Let's crack a barrel of cider and toast the grand opening of the first and only store in the Henderson mercantile empire."

"I think I'll stay out here," Shannon said. "When the customers start coming, I want to be around to make sure no one tries to discourage them from doing business with you."

All that afternoon, the new store did a brisk trade as the townspeople flocked in to purchase things that they had not been able to afford to buy in Cromwell's store for several weeks. The Cromwell men watching from across the street made no move to interfere, but Shannon knew that it was only a matter of time. From his position on the boardwalk outside the Henderson store, he could see that no one was going into Cromwell's store down the street, and that was a situation that Cromwell would not be likely to tolerate for long.

But the afternoon faded into evening, and when Kate Lipton closed up the store at sundown, there had been no incidents of any kind.

"Randy," Shannon said to Cutler as Kate was locking the door, "Miss Lipton and I are going to go get some supper. I want you to stand guard out here all evening. I'll relieve you later. If there's any trouble in the meantime, fire three shots into the air and I'll come."

"You and Randy can't guard the place forever, Clay," Kate Lipton said, as they walked together toward the café. "I'll be upstairs in my apartment all night, if there's any trouble."

"That's what I'm worried about," Shannon said. "I don't want you there alone when Cromwell does whatever it is he's going to do."

They ate a leisurely supper, and then Shannon escorted Kate Lipton back to the store. Randy Cutler was there, sprawled in a chair that was propped against the locked front door. He leaped up as Shannon and Kate Lipton approached.

"No problems, Mr. Shannon," Randy said.

"Thanks, Randy," Shannon said. "I'll stand by here.

Get some supper, then take a turn around the town just to see what's going on. Then drop back by and let me know how things look."

The sun had set now, and Shannon did not want to stay out on the boardwalk where he and Kate would be easy targets. Instead, they sat in the store's small office, talking about the store and its operation. The soft light of the oil lamps did nothing to lessen Kate Lipton's attractiveness, and before very long Shannon was finding it very hard to keep his mind on business matters. Kate had made some coffee, and at one point as the two of them reached for the coffee pot at the same time, their hands touched briefly. Shannon hurriedly withdrew his hand and let Kate pour the coffee, but their eyes met frequently now, and for some reason the conversation began to grow more personal.

At Kate's request, Shannon told her about his meeting with Cash Bonham and his days in Longhorn, when the trail herds were coming north every year. He told her other things too, about the years after Longhorn, about the cattle towns in which he had enforced the law and about the abrupt ending of his stay as the marshal of Stanleyville.

"It seems like such a shame—dismissing you after all you did for them," Kate said.

Shannon laughed.

"I'm twenty-nine years old, Miss Lipton," he said. "I've been a lawman for ten years, and in that ten years I've carried a star in eleven different towns. It's the same for all of us in my profession—the "decent" people call us when they need us, and send us on our way when the need no longer exists. You don't put down roots when you follow this way of life."

"That's rather sad, isn't it?" Kate Lipton mused. "Don't you get discouraged at times?"

"Sometimes," Shannon admitted. "But it's the life I've chosen, and I accept it. When I'm no longer needed here in Cauldron County, the same thing will happen—I'll be asked to move on."

"I hope not," Kate Lipton said in a soft voice. "I mean, this was a good place to live before Cromwell started all the trouble. "Perhaps it will be again, and you'll decide to stay."

"Perhaps," Shannon said. "What about you? It's been a hard time for you, surely."

Kate told Shannon about the ranch that she and her uncle had built up from nothing, only to see it lost when Tom Lipton was found dead and her ranch hands quit, forcing her to sell.

"It was Cromwell, of course," she said bitterly. "He ran them all away after Tom died. And his death was no accident, Mr. Shannon. Tom was a fine horseman, and that horse was the best and steadiest we had. My uncle was murdered, and everyone in the county knows it. Can you do anything about it, do you think?"

"I'll find a way," Shannon said. "That's a promise."

Their discussion was interrupted as three quick shots rang out through the streets.

"Randy?" Kate asked.

"Could be," Shannon said, jumping up. "Lock the door behind me and don't let anyone in."

"Be careful," Kate Lipton said. "Please."

Shannon ran down the main street, searching for the sound of the shots. Randy Cutler appeared, running toward him, his hat gone and his gun in his hand.

"Someone's busted into the home of Jason Taylor— you know, Mr. Henderson's lawyer. I was passing by his house and saw the door standing open with the glass broken in."

"Are Taylor and his wife all right?"

"No. They're inside. Someone beat them up and left them there. Mrs. Taylor is hysterical and her husband is unconscious. I sent someone for the doctor."

Doctor Evans was working on Taylor when Shannon and Randy came in. Mrs. Taylor was seated in a nearby chair, holding a bloody towel against her head and crying.

"Who did this, Mrs. Taylor?" Shannon asked, kneeling beside her.

"She says she didn't recognize them," the doctor said, cleaning a cut on Taylor's cheek. "Beat these folks up pretty good, whoever they were. The woman's got at least one cracked rib, and Taylor has a concussion, maybe worse."

"Well, what's the problem here?" said a voice from the doorway. A tall, heavy man with unkempt hair and tiny, glittering black eyes set deep in his puffy face was standing there, surveying the scene with a contemptuous smile. There was a cheap-looking star pinned crookedly on his wrinkled and sweat-stained shirt.

"Mr. Shannon," the doctor said with heavy irony, "meet Wade Stitch, our new town marshal. Mr. Stitch, meet Clay Shannon, our new county sheriff. I hope one of you intrepid lawmen is going to find the people who did this to the Taylors. Or am I being overly optimistic?"

"You got here pretty fast, Stitch," Shannon said. "Somebody must have called you right after it happened. Or did you have a premonition and get an early start?"

Stitch leaned comfortably against the doorframe.

"Very funny, Shannon," he said. "I can see that you're gonna be a real bundle of laughs. Well, since I'm here, let's have a little talk. I'm the town marshal, so this is under my jurisdiction. You ain't got no business interfering."

"There are two answers to that, Stitch," Shannon said. "First, if you knew anything about the law, you'd know that the county sheriff has jurisdiction throughout the county, including within the town limits. Second, you've got no business wearing that star, in this town or anywhere else. You're nothing but a hoodlum with a badge that your boss bribed and threatened the town council into giving you. So stay out of my way. I'm going to clean up this county, and I'll be perfectly happy to use you and your gunslinging friends as mops."

Shannon had expected an explosion from the gunman, or at least some sign of anger, but instead Stitch laughed lightly and settled more comfortably in the doorway.

"No need to be hard-nosed about this," Stitch said. "The county's big enough for both of us. Let's go down to the saloon and have a drink, talk it over, get things straight between us."

Shannon stood up and walked toward the door.

"Sorry," he said. "Maybe some other time. Right now I've got work to do."

He tried to push past Stitch, but the latter didn't move.

"Just one drink," Stitch suggested. "Do you good to relax awhile."

The boom of a shotgun filled the night.

"That came from the direction of the store!" Randy Cutler cried.

Of course it did, Shannon thought. *This was nothing but a decoy to get us out of the way. They're after the store.*

"What should we do, Mr. Shannon?" Randy asked, his voice shaking.

"This, for a start," Shannon replied. He drew the six-gun from his holster and brought it down hard on the crown of Wade Stitch's head. Stitch crumpled to the floor and lay there, out cold. Shannon grabbed his leg and dragged him out of the doorway.

"Come on," he said to Cutler. "Run!"

As they approached Henderson's store, Shannon could see that one of the new plate glass windows was broken, and by the light of the store's oil lamps he could also see that the interior of the store was in disarray, goods thrown about and counters overturned. Shannon felt the cold grip of terror. Someone had ransacked the store, and as he realized this, panic flooded through him. What had the intruders done to Kate Lipton?

His question was quickly answered. As he raced up onto the boardwalk, the shotgun boomed again, and in the muzzle flash Shannon saw a man come hurtling backward through the remaining window, scattering glass across the boardwalk as he fell. He lay squirming on the walk, holding his shoulder and screaming loudly. The door of the store opened, and Kate Lipton walked out, shoving two more shells into the chambers of the double-barreled shotgun she was holding. Her hair was tousled and she was breathing heavily, but Shannon could see no visible sign of injury to her.

"Are you all right?" he cried, grasping her by the shoulders and looking into her face.

"Yes," Kate replied, "but that one on the boardwalk isn't, and there's another one inside that's in even worse shape."

Shannon heard shouts, and saw that people were running along the street toward them.

"Randy, take care of this clown," Shannon said, pointing to the man who lay writhing on the sidewalk.

"If he tries to get up, shoot him. Come on, Kate, let's get inside."

The other victim of Miss Lipton's shotgun lay sprawled in the remains of a torn bag of flour. The buckshot had hit him square in the chest.

"Nice shooting," Shannon said with professional appreciation. "What happened?"

"They broke in as soon as you were out of sight and began to smash everything. I warned them to get out, but this one pulled a gun and came toward me. I took the shotgun out from under the counter and fired. The other one started after me and I got him with the second barrel."

She looked around.

"What a mess," she said. "And after all that work we did getting the place fixed up."

"It'll be fixed up again by tomorrow noon," Shannon said. He looked closely at Kate Lipton, and saw that she was now calm and that the hand that replaced the shotgun on the counter was rock-steady.

"Weren't you frightened?" Shannon asked, marveling at her coolness.

"Yes," she said, "but this isn't the first time I've ever killed a man, and if I'm going to keep running this store, I've got a feeling it won't be the last. Well, let's get to work, shall we? We open at eight in the morning, and we've a long night ahead of us."

Shannon could only stare at her, lost in admiration.

Chapter Seven
Retribution

At precisely eight A.M. Kate Lipton opened the Henderson General Store for business. She, Randy Cutler, and Shannon had worked through the night to repair the damage. Only after everything was in order did Kate retire to her apartment to comb her hair and change her dress. She came back downstairs looking as cool and composed—and as lovely—as ever.

Amazing, Shannon thought. *In the past eight hours, the woman's killed one man, wounded another, cleaned up a wrecked store, and gone without a night's sleep, yet she looks like she's just stepped off the cover of one of those eastern fashion magazines.*

Curt Henderson came galloping up to the front of the store on a lathered horse. Four of his men were following him.

73

"I just heard what happened," he said. "Is everyone all right?"

"Not quite," Shannon said. "Jason Taylor and his wife were beaten up, one of Cromwell's men is occupying a pine box at the undertaker's, another is in Doc's office getting the buckshot pried out of his hide, and Wade Stitch has a very bad headache. Other than that, everything's fine."

"Maybe not so fine," Randy Cutler said, gazing up the street. "Here comes trouble."

Wade Stitch and three other men were advancing down the street toward them. Shannon noted with satisfaction that Stitch had a bandage wound around his head.

"Good morning, Marshal," Shannon said pleasantly. "To what do we owe the honor of this visit? I trust that you've come to tell us that you've caught the brave fellows who beat up the Taylors last night."

"This ain't funny, Shannon," Stitch said, pulling out his revolver. "You and that Lipton woman are both under arrest."

"Oh?" Shannon said. "I don't recall spitting on the sidewalk, and I'm sure Miss Lipton hasn't."

"No more jokes, funny man," Stitch said. "Me and my deputies here are taking both of you into custody."

"No, you're not, Stitch," Shannon said in a low voice. "I don't feel like being arrested today, especially not by the likes of you, and if anyone touches Miss Lipton, I'll shoot them down without the slightest hesitation. Do I make myself clear?"

His hand moved close to the ivory handles of his Colt and he paused, waiting. Stitch hesitated, looking around at Randy Cutler, Curt Henderson, and Henderson's men.

"I ain't scared of your peach-fuzz deputy," he said, "but I ain't gettin' into no gunfight with the whole Henderson ranch."

"Mr. Henderson," Shannon said, "I want you and your men to stay out of this. You too, Randy. Keep your guns holstered, all of you. If Stitch gets me, walk away. So, Stitch, it's just you and me, and you've already got a gun in your hand. You ought to be able to take me. The question is—do you want to find out?"

Stitch stood stock still, eyeing the Colt and then looking up at Shannon, uncertainty on his face.

"Use it or put it away," Shannon said.

Stitch lowered the muzzle of his revolver and slid the weapon back into its holster.

"This ain't over, Shannon," he grunted. "Come on, boys, let's go see Mr. Cromwell."

"Give him my regards," Shannon said. "Tell him next time he'd better send real men to do the job."

Henderson pulled out a handkerchief and mopped his forehead.

"That was close," he said. "I though he was going to shoot you."

"It wouldn't have mattered if he'd tried," Shannon said. "He hadn't even cocked his six-gun. I'd have killed him where he stood."

Henderson shook his head in wonder.

"You amaze me, Shannon," he said. "You're the coolest customer I've ever come across."

"No, I'm not," Shannon said. "The coolest customer you'll ever meet is standing right beside you."

Henderson blinked.

"Miss Lipton?" he said. "What did she do?"

Shannon told him.

"So what's next?" Henderson said. "I can put some of my men to guarding the store, but we can't protect it forever."

"We may not have to," Shannon said. "Some smart general once said that the best defense is a good offense, and I've got one in mind. But first, I'm tired of playing this little charade of Stitch being town marshal. That's a phoney, and everyone knows it. Cromwell scared your friends on the town council into giving him that silly looking badge, and I'm betting they can be persuaded to take it back."

"How?" Henderson said.

"Can you get the town council together in the mayor's office in thirty minutes?"

"Yes, I suppose so. What have you got in mind?"

"Watch," Shannon said.

The special meeting of the Cauldron City council convened in the mayor's office a half hour later. The council members looked distinctly unhappy about being there, the mayor most of all.

"See here, Curt," the mayor was saying. "You ain't on the council and you can't call a meeting whenever you want to."

"He didn't call it, Mayor," Shannon said. "You did."

"I did?" the mayor said, confused.

"Yes. Try to keep that in mind. Now bring the council to order, please."

Grudgingly, the mayor fumbled in his desk drawer, found his gavel, and declared the town council to be in session.

"Now," Shannon said, "a few days ago, you folks appointed a town marshal. However, the appointment was illegal."

"Illegal?" said the mayor. "We all voted on it. Look, Shannon, we don't want Stitch around any more than you do, but . . ."

"But you were told that if you didn't appoint him, something would happen to you or to your families or your homes, right?"

"Yes, that's exactly what happened. But that's why we can't fire him—Cromwell would kill us."

"You don't have to fire him," Shannon said. "His appointment was null and void from the moment it was made. It was coerced, and that makes it invalid."

"But . . ."

"Besides that," Shannon continued, "the appointment was never completed."

"What do you mean?"

"Who swore Stitch in?"

"Why," said the mayor, "nobody."

"Who gave him the badge?"

The mayor was sweating profusely now.

"Nobody gave it to him," he said. "He made it himself. We didn't have a marshal's badge because we never had a town marshal before."

"Exactly," Shannon said. "Coercion, no swearing in, no official badge, therefore no marshal. The appointment was a complete legal nullity. Stitch is not, and never was, town marshal."

"Try telling that to Stitch or Cromwell," one of the council members said. "They're not too big on technical points of law."

"Very well, gentlemen, if legal arguments won't convince you, then let's try this method," Shannon said, drawing the Colt. He opened the loading gate and slowly spun the cylinder, dropping the shells out into the palm of his hand. "Some men only carry five rounds in the cylinder of these single action revolvers, so the hammer always rests on an empty chamber. But I always carry it fully loaded—six rounds. As you see, I've just taken five out," he said, holding up five cartridges for the councilmen to see. "That means there's one shell left in the gun." He spun the cylinder again and closed the loading gate.

"Now," he said, "we're going to resolve this in a manner that Cromwell will understand perfectly." He pointed the six-gun at the mayor and cocked the hammer. "Mayor," he said, "do you vote to fire Wade Stitch as town marshal?"

"I can't," the mayor protested. "I told you, Cromwell will . . ."

Shannon pulled the trigger. The hammer fell on an empty chamber.

"What are you doing?" the mayor squeaked.

Shannon cocked the hammer again, still pointing the revolver at the mayor's chest.

"I repeat, do you vote to fire Wade Stitch as town marshal?"

"Now look, Shannon, you can't . . ."

Shannon pulled the trigger again, and again the hammer fell on an empty chamber.

"Your chances are down to one in four, Mayor," Shannon said. "What's your answer?"

"Yes! Yes!" the mayor cried. "Stitch is out! He's out!"

Shannon cocked the hammer and pointed the gun at the council member sitting next to the mayor.

"What about you?" Shannon said. "What's your name?"

"G-G-Grover," the man stammered, staring wide-eyed down the barrel of the Colt.

"Well, Mr. Grover, is Stitch in or out?"

"This is intolerable!" Grover shouted. "You're crazy!"

The hammer fell again, but the gun did not fire.

"One in three," Shannon said. "The odds are getting

short, gentlemen. I'll ask you again, Mr. Grover—is he in or out?"

He cocked the hammer very slowly. The clicking of the cylinder was loud in the silent room.

"Out!" cried Grover. "He's out!"

"You?" Shannon said, swinging the muzzle to cover the third and final councilman.

"Out! Out!" the man squealed. "Put that gun away, for the love of heaven."

"Excellent," Shannon said, holstering the six-gun. "By a unanimous vote, the town council has revoked the appointment of Mr. Stitch as town marshal. Don't worry, gentlemen, I'll give him the news myself. Good day, friends."

He left them there, shaken and soaked in perspiration.

On the sidewalk outside the mayor's office, Shannon stopped to reload the Colt.

Henderson was staring at him in awe.

"What in the world were you doing, Clay?" he demanded. "You could have killed one of them. What if you'd hit the loaded chamber?"

"What loaded chamber?" Shannon asked in mock surprise.

"You took out five cartridges," Henderson said. "I counted them. You had one round left in the cylinder."

"Not exactly. You forgot to count the cartridge I removed before we went inside."

"You mean the gun was empty?"

"Completely."

Henderson began to laugh. He laughed so hard that it was several seconds before he could control himself again.

"So this is law and order," he said, wiping his eyes with his handkerchief.

"Let me tell you a secret, Mr. Henderson," Shannon said. "Before you can have law and order, you have to have justice, and sometimes you have to do strange things to achieve it. So, when the system doesn't work the way it's supposed to, when we're surrounded by lawlessness and disorder, we change the rules a little bit. We do what works."

"Well," Henderson said with a rueful grin, "what you did in there certainly worked, I'll say that for it."

"Yes, it worked," Shannon said, "but make no mistake—that silly little game we played in the mayor's office just now was only a prologue. Things are going to get very disagreeable now, and very, very dangerous."

Chapter Eight
The Silver Spur

"You're crazy, Clay," Henderson said. "You'll never get away with it."

"If we're going to break Cromwell's hold on the town, we have to take away his sources of income," Shannon replied.

"But the Silver Spur Saloon?" Henderson protested. "It would be like walking into the lions' den."

"I've closed up saloons before," Shannon said indifferently. "We know that Cromwell's making big money since he brought the gaming tables into the Silver Spur. We need to stop that. And since gambling's illegal in the county, it's my job as sheriff to uphold the ordinance and stop the gambling—one way or the other."

"But Cromwell's men hang around that place all the time," said Randy Cutler. "They'll shoot us full of holes if we try to shut the place down."

"Me, maybe," Shannon said. "Not you. You're not going, Randy. Neither are you, Mr. Henderson. Leave this to me."

"Clay, if you go in there alone, you'll be killed," Kate Lipton cried. "You've got to have some help."

"I won't risk any of your lives," Shannon said. "This is my job. The rest of you stay out of it. Do you hear me? *Stay out of it.* Wait for me at the sheriff's office. Kate, does the store have any axes in stock?"

Ten minutes later, Clay Shannon walked through the swinging doors of the Silver Spur Saloon. The room was occupied only by a sleepy bartender, two bored-looking saloon girls, and four men who were playing an indifferent game of penny-ante poker at a back table. The roulette wheels, faro layouts, and other gaming tables were deserted.

"Whatcha want, Sheriff?" the bartender said, eyeing the axe Shannon was carrying in his left hand.

"Are you married?" Shannon asked.

The bartender gaped at him.

"Uh, yeah, I am. Why?"

"Go home to your wife," Shannon replied, "unless you want her to be a widow. This saloon is closed, effective immediately."

"What?" the barman sputtered. "You can't close us down!"

"Bet I can," Shannon replied, walking over to the nearest roulette table.

He raised the axe high over his head and brought it down with all his strength on the tabletop. The wood splintered and the table collapsed onto the floor. The ivory ball from the roulette wheel bounced away across the floorboards.

Shannon walked to an adjacent faro table and dispatched it with two swift strokes of the axe, then started toward another roulette wheel.

The four men in the rear of the saloon had left their poker game and were hurrying forward toward Shannon. Simultaneously, the bartender came out from behind the bar holding a double-barreled shotgun.

"You better stop that, Shannon," he shouted. "Mr. Cromwell had these tables imported all the way from St. Louey."

"This equipment violates the county ordinance against gambling," Shannon replied, smashing another table. "That makes it contraband, and it's my duty as sheriff to destroy it."

"Mr. Cromwell said to stop anybody who tries to mess with the equipment," the bartender said, raising the shotgun.

"I'm not anybody," Shannon said. "I'm the sheriff, and it's not polite to point guns at sheriffs."

He swung the axe against the barrel of the shotgun, knocking it out of the bartender's grasp. The bartender staggered back, staring unbelievingly at his now-empty hands.

One of the four poker players started drawing his six-gun, and Shannon shifted the axe back to his left hand as the Colt magically appeared in his right.

"Do you own this saloon, brother?" he asked the man who was about to draw.

"Uh, no, I don't own it," the man said, his revolver still only halfway out of its holster.

"Then is it worth dying for?" Shannon inquired, cocking the Colt.

"No, *sir*," the man said, dropping his revolver back into the holster. "Not even close."

"Then get out—all of you," Shannon said. "You too, bartender. I don't want to see you in here again until I'm through with the place, understand?"

"Okay, okay, it ain't my saloon either," the bartender said, hastily following the poker players and the saloon girls out the swinging doors.

Shannon picked up the shotgun and shoved the weapon back out of sight under the bar. Then, methodically swinging the axe, he continued destroying the gaming tables one by one. He was in the process of splintering a particularly fancy roulette wheel when the creaking of a hinge warned him that someone was coming through the swinging doors behind him. He drew his six-gun and whirled to cover the doorway. To his amazement, Curt Henderson and Randy Cutler were there, each carrying an axe.

"What are you doing here?" Shannon demanded, uncocking the Colt. "I told you to wait for me. Get out of here before Cromwell's gunmen get wind of this and come looking for trouble."

Curt Henderson shook his head.

"We took a vote and decided it wasn't right for you to have to do this all by yourself," he said. "Anyway, this is partly my fight, remember?"

"But it's my *job,*" Shannon said. "The risk goes with the star. I don't want you two involved."

"It's my job too," Cutler said stubbornly, touching the deputy's badge on his chest.

"Now that we've settled that," Henderson said, "let's get to work."

He walked around behind the bar and started smashing the bottles of liquor on the shelves, while Randy Cutler began wielding his axe against one of the remaining faro tables.

A thought struck Shannon and he looked around, half-expecting to see Kate Lipton walking through the door also.

"Where's Miss Lipton?" he asked.

"She's standing guard outside," Henderson replied, sweeping a row of bottles off a shelf and onto the floor in a cascade of broken glass. "She'll warn us if any of Cromwell's people turn up before we're done here."

Shannon swore under his breath. Were all of these people deaf? He had expressly told Henderson not to get involved, and he had wanted to keep Randy Cutler and Kate Lipton out of harm's way as well. Instead, they were all risking their own lives to help him. Well, it was too late now. The die was cast, and whatever would happen, would happen. The best chance of minimizing the danger to everyone was to finish the job quickly.

While Randy Cutler was destroying the last of the gaming tables, Shannon moved around behind the bar with his axe and began to break in the heads of the beer barrels beneath the counter. The beer gushed out over the floor of the saloon, the froth mixing with the dirty sawdust and old cigarette butts that littered the boards. Wading through the muck, Shannon went to work wrecking the now-empty bar shelves. Then, just as he finished splintering the mirror behind the bar, Kate Lipton came hurrying into the saloon.

"Clay, they're coming," she said. "It's Stitch and four or five of his men."

Shannon frowned. This was exactly what he had hoped would not happen.

"Get out the back door, all of you," he said. "Hurry."

Even as he spoke, he heard heavy footfalls on the boardwalk outside the saloon.

"Too late," Kate said. "They're right outside."

"Then get down behind the bar, all three of you. And stay down, out of the way."

Henderson started to protest.

"I didn't build up the biggest cattle ranch in the county by hiding from trouble," he growled.

"I know that, Mr. Henderson," Shannon said, "but this is no time for arguments. Just do as I ask—*please*. I'll handle this."

Reluctantly, Henderson, Cutler, and Kate Lipton crouched down behind the bar.

Shannon tossed his axe into a corner, drew his six-gun again, and faced the door, waiting. Within seconds, Wade Stitch and five other Cromwell men came crowding through the door. They stared around in astonishment at the wreckage of the saloon.

"Come in, gentlemen," Shannon said. "I'm afraid I can't offer you a drink, but there are a couple of chairs left that I haven't gotten around to yet. Have a seat."

"Are you out of your mind, Shannon?" Stitch howled. "Cromwell's going to kill both of us for this."

"He might kill *you*," Shannon said. "Unless, of course, I kill you first."

Stitch had been reaching for his revolver as Shannon uttered these words. Once again, confronted with the unwavering muzzle of Shannon's Colt, he hesitated.

"You have a lot of trouble making up your mind about things, Stitch," Shannon said. "Every time I give you a chance to back up your big talk, you seem to get a cramp in your gun hand."

Stitch was now recovering from his surprise, and fury was taking its place.

"I've taken all I'm going to take from you, Shannon," he bellowed. "There are six of us, and you can't outshoot us all. Ready, boys?"

Shannon braced himself. He knew he could get Stitch, and probably at least one or two of the others, but six-to-one was heavy odds. He had not counted on such a fast reaction to his invasion of the saloon, and now he was about to pay for his miscalculation. *Sorry, everyone,* he thought. *I guess I'm losing my touch. Looks like I'm about to lose everything else too.*

"The first one of you who pulls a pistol gets a load of buckshot in the belly," said a deep voice from the side of the room. The startled Cromwell men looked around and saw that Curt Henderson and Randy Cutler had risen from behind the bar and were covering them, Cutler with his revolver and Henderson with a double-barreled shotgun. Kate Lipton stood beside them, her face pale but determined.

"Nice of the owner to keep a scattergun under the bar," said Henderson in a conversational tone. "It's loaded, too, in case you fellas are wondering."

"Well, Stitch," Shannon said, "looks like you and your friends don't have quite the edge you thought you had."

Stitch and his men looked first at Shannon, then at the weapons Henderson and Cutler were holding, and then at each other. The distress on their faces was almost comical.

"Decision time, boys," Shannon said. "Draw 'em or drop 'em."

Reluctantly, angrily, one by one, they undid their gunbelts and dropped them on the floor.

"Collect the guns, Randy," Shannon said. "Now, Stitch, take your hired gorillas and go tell Mr. Cromwell that he's out of the saloon business as of now. If he wants to start a church or an orphanage in this building, that's fine by me, but any attempt to reopen this establishment as a saloon will be regarded by me as an unfriendly act, and treated accordingly."

With red faces and deep scowls, Cromwell's men filed out of the saloon. As he reached the door, Stitch looked back at Shannon, his piglike eyes mean and menacing.

"You're dead," Shannon, he said. *"Dead."*

"Take your mouth and go home, Stitch," Shannon said. "I'm tired of listening to it flap."

Chapter Nine
Vengeance

Shannon herded Curt Henderson, Randy Cutler, and Kate Lipton out of the wrecked saloon and back to the sheriff's office.

"I appreciate what you did back there, all of you," Shannon said, "but you've put yourselves in great danger by doing it."

"It was fun," Randy Cutler said. "Besides, we got away with it."

"The whole town will be talking about what you did in the saloon," Kate Lipton said, her eyes shining. "You made them turn tail and run. It was marvelous."

"Let's not start celebrating too soon," Shannon said. "The only reason we're all still in one piece is that so far Wade Stitch hasn't had the sand for a stand-up fight. But we can't count on that happening again. We've backed him down twice in front of his own men, and nobody, particularly a professional gunman like Stitch, can afford that. Next time he'll fight."

"So what happens now?" Henderson asked.

"They'll strike back," Shannon said. "You can count on it. Stitch is probably on his way out to Cromwell's ranch to tell him about it right now. Cromwell's going to be furious."

"Do you think they'll try to hit our store again?" Kate asked.

"Perhaps, but I doubt it—not for the moment, at least. They know that if they did, we could do the same to them. My guess is they'll come at us some other way."

"What do you suggest we do?" Henderson asked.

"Go back to your ranch and stay there," Shannon said. "And I mean *stay there.* Keep Todd and Sarah there too, and enough hands to protect the place. I don't think they'd try to attack the house directly, but Cromwell and Stitch might just be angry enough or crazy enough to do it."

"What if they go after my cattle?"

"I hope they do," Shannon said. "We've nearly put him out of business here in town, and now it's time to run him out of the county as well. If I can catch his men with a herd of stolen cattle, that should be enough to finish him."

He turned to Kate Lipton.

"Kate," he said, "until we see what's going to happen

next, I think you'd better close up the store, gather up your personal things, and go somewhere else for a while. Is there anywhere you can stay for a few days?"

"She can come out to the ranch with me," Henderson said. "Sarah would be glad for the company."

"Good," Shannon said. "Get going as quickly as you can. Randy, I want you to stand by here in the office. Keep the door locked and don't let anyone in except me. I'll bring you back some supper."

"What are you going to do?" Kate asked anxiously.

"I'm going to take a little walk around the town," Shannon said. "If something's going to happen, I want to know about it before it starts, not afterward."

"Can't I come along?" Randy said.

"No, pal, I want you right here so that I can find you if I need you. Come on, Kate, I'll walk you back to the store to get your things."

"A couple of my men came into town with me," Henderson said. "I'll round them up and meet you at the store. We'll load some supplies into the wagon and head for the Diamond Seven."

"All right," Shannon said, "but make it as fast as you can. Wade Stitch is probably halfway to Cromwell's ranch by now, and I want all of you out of harm's way before they have a chance to decide what to do."

A half-hour later, Henderson's ranch hands had finished loading up their wagon and were ready to leave town.

"Your men aren't armed," Shannon said to Henderson.

"No, I didn't want to chance any gunplay while they were here in town," the rancher replied. "Like I said before, my men are cowhands, not gunhands."

"All the more reason for you to get them and yourself back to the Diamond Seven quickly. Here's Miss Lipton now."

Kate Lipton came out of the store carrying a small valise and some other items. Shannon took them and put them in the back of the wagon, then turned to help Kate up onto the seat. As she took his outstretched hand, she hesitated.

"Be careful, Clay," she said in a small voice. "You worry about the rest of us, but you'll be the one in the greatest danger."

"Don't worry," Shannon said, laughing. "I'm practically indestructible."

"Maybe," Kate said, "but you're not bulletproof. So be careful."

She kissed him firmly on the cheek and then climbed onto the wagon seat beside one of the Diamond Seven ranch hands. The other man got into the back of the wagon with the supplies. Curt Henderson mounted his horse and followed the wagon as it pulled away.

Shannon watched the wagon until it was out of sight, then turned and walked back toward the sheriff's office. He could not free himself of a feeling of unease, a faint but tangible sense of foreboding. He checked the office to be sure that Randy Cutler had locked himself in as instructed.

"Everything all right?" Randy asked.

"I hope so," Shannon said. "I surely hope so."

Shannon had not eaten anything that day, so he headed for the café to get something for himself and the deputy. As he approached the café, he was startled to see Arch Cromwell and his sister, Marian, walking along the boardwalk toward him. As they drew near him, Arch Cromwell gave him a wintry smile.

"Well, Sheriff," he said, "it looks like you've won this round. I saw what you did to the Silver Spur. Quite a mess. Congratulations."

Shannon mumbled a reply, but his mind was working furiously. Cromwell was in town, not at his ranch, which meant that he must have heard about the destruction of the saloon within a few minutes of its happening. Yet he was displaying no anger, uttering no recriminations. *What's going on here?* Shannon thought. *He ought to be foaming at the mouth, but instead he's acting like a man out for a Sunday stroll. It just isn't normal—not for him, anyway.*

"Where's your friend Stitch?" Shannon asked. "In some dark alley waiting to shoot me in the back?"

"Oh," Cromwell said carelessly, "when he told me about the way you faced him down in the saloon, I ordered him to go back to the ranch and stay out of trouble for a while. You've certainly got him buffaloed,

Sheriff. I don't think you'll have any more trouble with him."

They had arrived together at the front door of the café.

"Marian and I were just going in to have a bite to eat," Cromwell said. "Why don't you join us?"

Shannon stared at him, still perplexed by Cromwell's calm acceptance of Shannon's foray into the saloon and this inexplicable invitation.

He's up to something, Shannon thought, *but what? Some sort of bribe attempt, I'll bet.*

"Yes, please do join us, Sheriff," Marian Cromwell said. "It would be nice if we could all be friends."

Lady, Shannon thought, *you may mean what you say, but I'd rather make friends with a rattlesnake than with your brother.*

Yet in the end his curiosity overcame both his astonishment and his distrust. *If nothing else,* he decided, *I'll be able to keep an eye on Cromwell for a little while, and it'll be interesting to hear his proposition. Sorry, Randy, you'll have to wait a bit for your dinner.*

But the meal produced no startling revelations. Cromwell remained civil while they were eating, but said very little. He seemed preoccupied, and Shannon, never much of a conversationalist, found himself half-listening to Marian Cromwell's chatter about matters that were both bland and trivial. The only information he gleaned that was of any interest was that the

Cromwells were planning to spend the night in town, and had taken rooms at the hotel.

Finally, Shannon could bear the discomfort of the situation no longer, and excused himself on the grounds that he had to get back to relieve his deputy. He left the café and started toward the office, carrying a covered dish with Cutler's supper and pondering the seemingly incredible meeting with Arch Cromwell.

As he neared the office, he heard the sound of a galloping horse coming full-tilt along the street in the gathering twilight. He stepped back against the wall outside the office and drew the Colt as the horseman approached. The rider, whoever it was, was calling out loudly as he brought the lathered horse to a halt a few yards away.

"Sheriff!" the man cried. "Sheriff Shannon!"

Shannon recognized one of the ranch hands who had ridden out of town with Curt Henderson and Kate Lipton.

"I'm right here, cowboy," Shannon said. "What is it?"

The rider slid off the horse and went to one knee in the street, then lurched to his feet and staggered toward Shannon. In the lamplight coming from the windows of the sheriff's office, Shannon saw that there was blood on his shirt.

"Come quick!" he gasped, falling to the boardwalk in front of Shannon. "Hurry!"

As Shannon pulled the fallen hand into a sitting position, he saw that the man was bleeding from a wound in his side.

"All right, cowboy, take it easy," Shannon said. "Now tell me—*what's wrong?*"

"They got Henderson," the man gasped.

"What?" Shannon said, grabbing him by his shirt front. "What are you talking about?"

"They jumped us on the road back to the Diamond Seven. Five or six of 'em. Rode out of the rocks and stopped the wagon. Henderson tried to make a fight of it, but they shot him right out of his saddle. He never got his pistol out of the holster."

"You're sure Henderson's dead?"

"Yeah. They must have plugged him ten or twelve times. Kept firing into his body after he was on the ground."

Shannon felt a wave of nausea sweeping over him.

"What about Miss Lipton?" he said hoarsely.

"They knocked her down when she tried to help Henderson, but she's all right. They didn't shoot her. They just laughed at her and rode away."

"Who was it? Who did the shooting?"

"It was Stitch and some of the Cromwell men. We never had a chance, Sheriff. Roy and I did our best, but we didn't have no guns, and they just opened up on us."

"I understand. How far out of town was this?"

"Not far—couple of miles maybe."

"What happened to your other man?"

"Roy was hurt, but he got on Mr. Henderson's horse

and headed for the Diamond Seven to tell them what had happened."

"And you left Miss Lipton out there on the road *alone?*" Shannon roared.

"It was what she wanted," the ranch hand cried. "She told me to unhitch one of the wagon horses and ride back to town to find you. I just did what she said. You gotta come quick, Sheriff."

Shannon eased the wounded man to the walk.

"Randy," he called, "get out here!"

Cutler came out the door with a rifle in his hands.

"I heard the commotion," he said. "What's happened?"

"Henderson and Kate were ambushed on the road to the Diamond Seven. This man's hurt—help me get him inside."

They stretched the wounded man out on the bunk in one of the jail cells.

"Get the doctor," Shannon said. "I'm going after Kate."

As Cutler ran out of the office, Shannon bent down beside the ranch hand.

"You're *sure* this was Stitch and Cromwell's men?" he asked.

"Yeah, it was them all right. They didn't have no masks on or nothin', and there was still plenty of light left. I saw 'em plain. Am I hit bad?"

"You'll be all right," Shannon said, checking the wound. "Just nicked a rib. Cutler will be back with the doctor in a minute. When he gets here, tell him to get some men and follow me out there as quickly as he can."

"They was laughing, Sheriff," the ranch hand said in a voice choked with emotion. "Stitch and them was *laughing* while they killed Mr. Henderson."

"Don't worry," Shannon said grimly. "They won't be laughing for very long."

It was well after dark by the time Shannon reached the location of the ambush, but the moon was nearly full and by its light Shannon saw the wagon and the one remaining horse standing in the road long before he reached them. Kate Lipton was sitting in the roadway beside Henderson's body. As Shannon swung off the buckskin, she got up and ran to him. Shannon could see that she had been crying.

He stood there with his arms around her, looking over her shoulder at the huddled form on the ground that had been Curt Henderson. The ranch hand had been right—Henderson had been shot at least a dozen times.

"Why, Clay?" Kate sobbed. "Why?"

Shannon knew why, and now he knew how the tragedy had come about. Because Arch Cromwell had been in town instead of at his ranch, he had learned of the saloon incident from Stitch almost immediately, and undoubtedly would have guessed that Henderson would be heading out of town for the Diamond Seven.

The rest had been simple—a few quick orders to Stitch to ambush Henderson on the road, and then off to dinner. *And I provided Cromwell with an ironclad alibi,* Shannon told himself. *Dining with the sheriff while murder was being done on the road. Perfect.* As Shannon stood there in the bloodied roadway, with Curt Henderson lying dead at his feet and Kate Lipton sobbing in his arms, he felt as if he were drowning in a sea of rage and grief—and searing, soul-destroying humiliation.

Shannon had just gotten a blanket out of the wagon and spread it over Curt Henderson's body when Randy Cutler arrived with several men he had gathered into an impromptu posse. At almost the same moment, the sound of hooves and the glimmer of lanterns heralded the approach of a group of horsemen coming from the opposite direction. Shannon thought for a moment that Stitch and his men might have returned, but instead Todd Henderson and a half-dozen of the Diamond Seven hands rode up. The younger Henderson dismounted and ran over to the wagon.

"Give me some light here," he said to one of the men who was carrying a lantern. Then he pulled the blanket away and stared down in anguish at his father's shattered body. A murmur of dismay went up from the Diamond Seven men as they saw what had been done to their employer.

"Was it Cromwell?" Todd Henderson croaked.

"Your cowhand says it was Wade Stitch and some of Cromwell's men," Shannon replied.

With a cry of rage, Todd Henderson threw down the blanket and leaped onto his horse. Shannon grabbed the bridle.

"Wait, Todd," he said. "Where are you going?"

"To Cromwell's ranch," Todd replied. "I'm going to get him for this."

"Cromwell's not at his ranch, he's in town staying at the hotel," Shannon said. "And besides, Stitch did the shooting, not Cromwell."

"Cromwell gave the orders," Todd Henderson snarled, "and I'm going to make him pay for it."

He jerked the horse's head around, breaking Shannon's grip on the bridle. Spurring the horse into a gallop, he disappeared into the darkness toward the town. The other Diamond Seven riders started to follow him, but Shannon blocked the way.

"Hold it, men," Shannon said. "I'll go after Todd. The rest of you help Deputy Cutler put Mr. Henderson's body in the wagon, and then get him and Miss Lipton back to the Diamond Seven."

He swung into the saddle and sent the buckskin charging down the road. The buckskin was fast, but Todd Henderson's horse was fast also, and it was immediately apparent to Shannon that he could not catch Henderson before he reached the town.

That young fool, he thought. *Guess I can't blame him much, though. I'd probably do the same if I were him.*

As he galloped into town he caught sight of Henderson pounding along the main street ahead of him. *I shouldn't have told him where Cromwell was,* Shannon thought. *I've got to catch him before he does something stupid.*

Henderson had already reined up in front of the hotel and started inside when Shannon arrived. As he hurried toward the hotel entrance, Shannon could see through the open doorway that Cromwell and his sister were just crossing the lobby, headed for the stairs. Todd Henderson was behind them, drawing his gun.

"Todd! Stop!" Shannon shouted, sprinting for the door.

"Turn around and take it like a man, Cromwell!" Todd yelled, raising his pistol.

Cromwell and his sister turned in surprise, and a look of sheer terror came over Cromwell's face as he saw Todd Henderson taking aim at him. Marian Cromwell began screaming. Cromwell quickly drew a derringer from his coat, pointed it at Todd Henderson, and pulled the trigger just as Henderson fired at him. The double report shook the walls of the hotel lobby, sending several other guests scrambling for cover. Todd Henderson dropped his revolver and staggered back as the bullet from the der-ringer struck his right arm. At the same time, Marian Cromwell gasped and collapsed to the floor, clutching her abdomen. Cromwell raised the derringer to fire a second shot at Todd Henderson, but by that time Shannon had charged across the lobby with his six-gun in his hand.

"Drop it, Cromwell!" he shouted. Cromwell let the derringer fall from his hand and stood gaping at his sister, who was now lying on her back on the carpet, unmoving.

"He's shot my sister!" Cromwell cried. "Somebody get the doctor!"

Shannon bent over her, and saw that there was nothing to be done.

"She's dead, Cromwell," Shannon said, straightening up. "I'm sorry."

Todd Henderson had dropped to his knees, holding his wounded arm and staring aghast at Marian Cromwell's body.

"I didn't mean to shoot *her*!" Henderson whimpered. "I was trying to hit Cromwell!"

"Too bad your aim wasn't better," Shannon said acidly.

Horses were arriving in front of the hotel, and Randy Cutler came into the lobby followed by the men of his posse. They gazed in appalled surprise at the hideous scene before them.

"Randy," Shannon said, "stay with Mr. Cromwell. Help him to take care of his sister's body. Then I want you back at the office as soon as possible."

Cromwell was still looking down in disbelief at the dead woman.

"He killed her!" Cromwell said. "That little skunk killed my sister! What are you going to do about this, Shannon?"

"What I have to," Shannon said sorrowfully. He turned to Todd Henderson.

"Todd," he said, "you're under arrest."

"But I didn't *mean* to kill her," Henderson wailed.

"No," Shannon said, "you didn't mean to, but you did. Let's go. I'll get someone to look at that arm when we get to the jail."

He took Todd Henderson by his good arm and led him out of the hotel lobby.

"Why are you arresting me?" Todd Henderson said. "Cromwell killed my father!"

"Marian Cromwell didn't," Shannon said, "but you killed her, and in the eyes of the law, that makes you just as much a murderer as Cromwell. Now let's go, and no more arguments. I want you safely locked up before Cromwell recovers from the shock and sends his gunmen after you."

An hour later, Randy Cutler returned to the jail. By that time, Shannon had locked Todd Henderson in a cell and was sitting at the desk in the office, contemplating the horrors of that long night. As the significance of the violent events of the past hours began to fully sink in, Shannon found himself overcome with a feeling of revulsion. Only that afternoon he had been enjoying his success at the saloon; now, just a few hours later, the elder Henderson had been butchered on the road a few scant miles from safety, an innocent woman was lying dead on the floor of a hotel lobby, and the younger

Henderson was in jail and under arrest for her murder. It was like some sort of nightmare. And Shannon knew there would be more to come. Much more, for the men who had so brutally assassinated Todd Henderson's father were still at large, and it would be up to Shannon to find them and bring them to justice.

Justice, he thought. *What justice can possibly come out of this? Nothing can ever make things right again. Nothing. And it's my fault. All of it. My fault.*

He put his head down on the desk and tried unsuccessfully to shut the brutal images of the evening out of his tortured mind.

Chapter Ten
A Form of Justice

Shannon sat at his desk all through the night, unable to sleep, waiting for the morning. As the gray light of dawn began to filter through the office window, he arose stiffly from the desk, slipped on his coat, took his rifle from the rack on the wall, and went outside to the little stable behind the jail. He was saddling the buckskin when Randy Cutler came hurrying out of the office, bleary-eyed and tousled. He had been sleeping on the bunk in one of the cells, unwilling to leave Shannon there in the office alone.

"Where are you going?" he asked, yawning.

"The Cromwell ranch," Shannon replied. "I'm going to bring in Wade Stitch."

"You can't go out there alone," Cutler said, suddenly wide awake. "Cromwell must have thirty men on his payroll. They'll cut you down before you get anywhere near Stitch."

"They may try," Shannon agreed.

"I'll get my coat and come with you," Cutler said.

"No, I want you to stay here and guard the jail. Cromwell might send men to try to kill Todd Henderson."

Kate Lipton came out the back door of the jail.

"I heard you talking out here," she said. "I just brought over some coffee for you two and Todd. It's inside. Come and have a cup."

"Mr. Shannon's going out to Cromwell's ranch to get Wade Stitch," Cutler told her. "Try to talk some sense into him, Miss Lipton. He wants to go alone."

Kate Lipton gave a little cry of alarm.

"Clay, you can't do that. At least go by the Diamond Seven and get some men to ride out there with you."

"If I rode up to Cromwell's ranch house with a bunch of Diamond Seven men, we'd have a bloodbath for certain," Shannon said. "It's better if I go by myself."

"It's insane, Clay. You'll be killed."

"I carry the star, Kate," Shannon said, "and there's a murderer to be arrested. That's my job—remember?"

Once more Shannon found himself approaching the gate of the Cromwell Ranch. Beneath the steer skull, the sign still read *Keep Out. Trespassers Will Be Shot.* Shannon leaned out of the saddle, unlatched the gate, and passed through. As he rode up the winding trail toward the ranch house, he braced himself for what was about to happen. He was under no illusions about the probable result.

"But don't worry, Mr. Henderson," Shannon said aloud to the ghost of Curt Henderson, "I'll get Stitch. Whatever happens, I'll get Stitch for you."

As the trail curved around a low hill, the ranch house came in sight. Out of the corner of his eye, Shannon saw two horsemen, both carrying rifles at the ready, take up positions a hundred yards on each side of him, riding with him toward the house. He ignored them.

More men were waiting on the porch of the house by the time he reached it. Stitch was nowhere in sight, but Shannon guessed that some of the men watching him from the porch had been among those who had ambushed Henderson the previous night. Their unfriendly eyes followed his every move as he dismounted and tied the buckskin to the hitchrail. As he stepped onto the porch, one of the men blocked his path.

"Where do you think you're goin', Shannon?" he asked.

"Around you or over you," Shannon replied. "Which way is up to you."

The front door of the house opened, and an old woman appeared in the doorway.

"Mister Cromwell says to let him in," she called out.

Grudgingly, the man confronting Shannon stepped aside to let him pass.

The living room of the house was large and dark. Although it was full daylight outside, the shutters were closed and only one lamp was lit. By its dim light, Shannon saw that Cromwell was lying on a leather couch in front of the fireplace, holding a wet cloth to his head.

"I've been expecting you, Shannon," Cromwell said in a thin voice. "Sorry I can't get up. I get these blinding headaches sometimes. They seem to be getting worse and worse. Are you after me?"

"I've come to arrest Wade Stitch," Shannon said. "He's been identified as the leader of the men who murdered Curt Henderson last night."

"I'm sorry about Henderson," said Cromwell with a grimace. "Believe it or not, I'm truly sorry. We could have worked something out. I know we could have. I wish last night hadn't happened."

Cromwell's voice broke, and to Shannon's amazement, he realized that Cromwell was actually crying. *What sort of man is this?* Shannon wondered. *He orders a murder and then breaks down and cries about it? Is it because he's upset about his sister's death?*

"Sorry or not, Cromwell," Shannon said, "Henderson's dead, and your pet thug Stitch is wanted for his murder. Will you call him in from wherever he's hiding, or do I have to go looking for him?"

Cromwell rose slowly from the couch, still pressing the cloth to his forehead.

"I'll bring him in," he said, "but whether he goes with you or not is up to him."

He turned and called out, wincing as he did so.

"Come on in, Stitch," he said. "You've got a visitor."

A door opened and Wade Stitch swaggered into the room, grinning.

"So you came to arrest me?" he said. "You're a real optimist, Shannon. What makes you think you'll ever leave this ranch alive?"

"If I don't, you won't," Shannon said. "Unbuckle your gunbelt and come quietly, and you may live to hang. Otherwise, Mr. Cromwell's going to have blood all over his living room."

"You don't scare me, Shannon," Stitch sneered. "You've got a big reputation with a gun, but I ain't exactly slow myself. I had to back off the last couple of times we met, but this time you're all by your lonesome, and I'm betting you ain't good enough to take me and still get through those men on the porch out there."

"Let's go, Stitch," Shannon said. "We've got a long ride into town."

"Not this time, law dog," Stitch grunted.

His hand flashed toward his holster and came up again, his thumb cocking the hammer of the six-gun as he drew it from the holster. Before the hammer had reached the full cocked position, the roar of Shannon's .45 rattled the windows of the room, and Stitch went over backward, a bullet in his chest. He rolled over on his side, still trying to bring the hammer of his revolver to full cock, but his grip weakened and he fell back, dropping the gun to the floor.

"I'll get you for this, Shannon," he wheezed.

"Not in this world, you won't," Shannon said.

Stitch tried to say something else, but his voice trailed off and his body went limp. The angry light in his eyes dimmed and vanished, leaving only a blank stare.

I wonder where the light in a man's eyes goes when he dies, Shannon thought. *It must go somewhere. I wonder where.*

Cromwell was gawking at the fallen man.

"Is he dead?" he whispered.

Shannon checked for a pulse, and found none.

"Yes," he said. "I guess he wasn't quite as fast as he thought he was."

The front door burst open and Stitch's men came crowding into the room, their weapons drawn. Cries of anger escaped them as they saw Wade Stitch lying on the floor. They pointed their guns at Shannon, and Shannon knew that in that moment he was standing on the knife edge of eternity.

"What about it, Cromwell?" Shannon said, leveling his six-gun at Cromwell. "They'll get me, but I'll get you first. That's a promise."

Cromwell sat back down on the couch and covered his face with the wet cloth.

"Let him go, boys," he said. "Stitch was a fool and he got what he deserved. Let Shannon go."

Slowly and reluctantly, the onlookers holstered their weapons, glancing angrily from Cromwell to Shannon and back again. Shannon holstered his own six-gun and started for the door.

Suddenly Cromwell leaped up from the couch, hurling the cloth away.

"All right, Shannon," he screamed, "you've got what you came for. You've killed my man. Now what about the scum that killed Marian? What about him?"

"He's in jail," Shannon said, "and he'll stay there until he goes on trial for shooting your sister."

"You come here and kill Stitch, and then you tell me that Henderson punk is going to sit in jail until some judge sets him free?" Cromwell shrieked. "That's not good enough, Shannon! It isn't good enough!"

"It's the law, Cromwell," Shannon said. "He'll stand trial. You have my word on it."

"He'll never stand trial!" Cromwell bawled. "Never! I'll see to that! He's going to pay for what he did!"

Shannon could hardly believe the transformation that had occurred in Cromwell. A few moments ago he was calmly telling his men to let Shannon leave unharmed, and now he was wild-eyed and screaming, his face purple with fury and spittle flying from his lips.

"Did you hear me, Shannon?" Cromwell shouted. His voice had become a shrill screech, and his whole body was shuddering as he raised his clenched fists in front of him and shook them violently at Shannon. "He's going to *pay,* I tell you! *Pay! Pay! Pay!*"

"I heard you the first time," Shannon said softly.

He turned and walked to the door. The watching gunmen parted to let him through. At the door, Shannon glanced back at Stitch's body, then looked once more at the trembling Cromwell.

"Good day, Mr. Cromwell," he said. "Sorry about the mess on your living room floor. The next time I come for somebody, I'll make the arrest outside."

Chapter Eleven
On the Edge

W hen Shannon arrived back at his office, he found Doctor Evans in the jail wrapping a new bandage around Todd Henderson's injured arm.

"I'm glad you're here, Doc," Shannon said. "I'd like to talk to you."

When the doctor had finished with Todd, he came into Shannon's office and closed the door behind him.

"What is it, Sheriff?" he asked. "Are you hurt?"

"No," Shannon said. "I just want some information. How much do you know about Arch Cromwell? About his behavior, I mean?"

"Pretty erratic, from what I hear," Evans said. "Loses his temper easily, as I understand it. Why?"

"Do you think it's possible that he's mentally ill?"

Evans frowned.

"I don't know much about mental illness," he said. "Nobody does, I guess, except some of those fancy experts back east and over in Europe. Still, I've always maintained that anyone who commits murder, or who orders it done, has to be considered mentally ill."

"I see your point," Shannon said, "but what possible explanation can there be for Cromwell's erratic conduct? We're talking about a man who's normal one minute and then goes into a screaming rage the next. He orders someone killed and a few hours later cries about it. This same man suffers from sudden, blinding headaches, which he says are getting worse. He literally seems to go crazy at a moment's notice. You should have seen him this morning—he was really in a bad way."

"Headaches, you say?" Evans asked. "And sudden fits of uncontrollable rage? I did see something like that once before, years ago in another town. I sent the man to a specialist in Chicago."

"And?"

"He had a brain tumor. There was nothing anybody could do for him. He died within weeks, raving mad."

The doctor had been gone only a few minutes when Sarah Henderson walked into Shannon's office. Her eyes were red from crying and there were dark circles underneath them.

"Why have you locked my brother up?" she demanded angrily.

"You know why, Miss Henderson," Shannon said. "He killed Cromwell's sister."

"It was an accident. He didn't mean to kill her. And Cromwell had our father killed last night. You haven't forgotten that, have you?"

"I'm not likely to forget it—ever," Shannon said. "As for it being an accident, your brother was trying to kill Arch Cromwell at the time, and even if Cromwell did order your father's death, that didn't give Todd the right to try to kill him. As much as I sympathize with Todd and with you, the fact remains that Todd shot an innocent woman while he was himself trying to commit murder. That makes Marian Cromwell's death manslaughter at the very least, and I have to hold Todd until a jury decides what to do about it. I'm sworn to uphold the law in Cauldron County, Miss Sarah, and that's what I intend to do."

"And what about Cromwell? Why don't you arrest him too?"

"I'll arrest him just as soon as I have enough evidence to make sure that he hangs for what he's done. If I bring him in now, he'll hire a dozen lawyers and walk out of jail without ever coming to trial."

"And you call that justice?"

"No," Shannon said, "I call that a total lack of justice. And that's exactly why I don't want to arrest Cromwell until I'm sure we can get a conviction."

"Then I'll kill Cromwell myself," the girl said, her voice breaking.

"Don't be a fool, Sarah," Shannon said. "Your brother's in jail because he tried to take the law into his own hands. Don't make the same mistake. We don't need any more Hendersons dead or sitting in those cells back there. So go back to the ranch and leave this to me. I'll get Cromwell, but I'll do it my way."

"Your way got my father killed," she said. "You'll probably get Randy killed too."

"Not if I can help it," Shannon replied. "When is your father's funeral?"

"Today," she said. "We're burying him in the family graveyard on the ranch this afternoon."

"I'll be there," Shannon said.

"No, you won't," Sarah spat. "You aren't invited, Mr. Shannon. If you come, I'll set the dogs on you. So just stay away from the Diamond Seven—you're not welcome there anymore."

Shannon was alone in the office that afternoon when Kate Lipton came in.

"I just got back from Mr. Henderson's funeral at the Diamond Seven," she said. "I heard that Sarah told you not to come. I'm sorry for that. It was wrong of her."

"I can't blame her for feeling the way she does," Shannon said. "Father dead, brother in jail—she's had a rough time."

"May I see Todd?" Kate asked. "I'd like to tell him about his father's burial, since he couldn't be there."

Shannon unlocked the door to the jail and let her in.

"I won't be long," she said. "When Randy gets back from the ranch, perhaps you and I can go and get some supper."

"I'd like that," Shannon said, "but I think I'd better stick close here. This thing is a long way from being over, and I don't want Randy here alone if there's trouble around the jail."

"I understand," Kate said. "I'll bring you both something to eat later."

Shannon went back to his desk and sat thinking. *There'll be trouble, all right,* he told himself. *The only question is, what kind?*

His answer was not long in coming. The sound of approaching horses alerted him, and he went out onto the boardwalk to investigate. A large group of Diamond Seven riders were nearing the jail, and they did not look very pleased. They reined up in front of the jail and sat there tensely in their saddles, eyeing Shannon with unconcealed animosity.

I wonder, Shannon thought, *if there's anybody left in this county who doesn't hate me.*

"What can I do for you, men?" he asked.

"We want you to let Todd Henderson go," said one of the riders. Shannon recognized the speaker as the Diamond Seven's foreman, Red Perkins.

"You know I can't do that, Red," Shannon replied. "Not until the circuit judge gets here, at least."

"You got no right to hold Todd," another rider said.

"Curt Henderson was a good man. The people who killed him deserve to die."

"One of them already has," Shannon pointed out.

"Yeah, we heard about you getting Stitch," Perkins said. "We thank you for that, Sheriff. But that don't change the fact that Todd's in jail and Cromwell is running around loose, and that ain't right."

"We could take Todd out of there without your say-so," a third ranch hand chimed in. "There're about twenty of us here, and you couldn't stop us."

"Maybe not," Shannon said, "but I'd have to try, and that would mean gunplay. There's been enough killing around here lately. Let's not have any more." Kate Lipton came out of the office and stood beside Shannon.

"I've just spoken with Todd," she said to the Diamond Seven hands. "He understands now that what he did was wrong, and he's willing to wait this out and trust the law to make Cromwell answer for his crimes. In the meantime, I'm going to bring Todd some tobacco and other things to make him more comfortable, and I'll help look after him while he's here. So please listen to the sheriff and do as he asks."

"There's something else you men need to consider," Shannon said. "Stitch is dead, but Cromwell's got about three dozen other gunslingers on his payroll, and he's already sworn to kill Todd for what Todd did to his sister. If I let Todd out, he'd be in great danger. Could you protect him from the entire Cromwell gang if they came after him?"

"I dunno," Perkins said. "Can you?"

"I can try," Shannon said. "Now, go on back to the Diamond Seven, all of you. Don't stay in town. I don't want any gunfights in the streets between you and Cromwell's men."

"We can take care of ourselves," Perkins said.

"No, you can't," Shannon retorted. "Cromwell's people are mostly professionals, hired guns who've killed before and won't hesitate to kill again. You men are working cowhands. You wouldn't last three minutes in a gunfight with them. Besides, a gun battle in the middle of town would mean that innocent people would get hurt. So please—go back to the ranch and let the law take its course. I'll get Cromwell. You can count on that."

The Diamond Seven men hesitated and then, with much muttering and grumbling, turned their horses and headed down the street out of town. When they were out of sight, Shannon smiled wanly at Kate Lipton.

"Thank you for backing me," Shannon said to her. "But please don't take that kind of chance again. If trouble had started, you could have gotten hurt."

"So could you," Kate said, her green eyes flashing.

"Yes," Shannon said, "but—"

"I know," Kate interrupted him. "It's your job. Now please come inside. I'll stay here with you until Randy gets back."

They went back into the office to wait. Neither of them had much to say, for the events of the past hours were weighing heavily on them. Still, even in the silence, Shannon found himself profoundly grateful for Kate's presence, and he was neither surprised nor sorry when she reached across the desk and wordlessly took his hand in hers, holding it tightly as they sat there alone in the gathering twilight.

Twenty minutes later Randy Cutler arrived. He had just returned from the Diamond Seven Ranch, dusty and tired.

"I met Red Perkins and his men on the road," he said. "They told me you asked them to go back to the ranch. They weren't very happy about it, but they went."

"Good," Shannon said. "Maybe we can keep this thing under control now."

"Shouldn't we have let a few of the Diamond Seven hands stay around here, just in case of trouble?" Cutler asked. "Cromwell's bound to try something."

"And I'm trying to keep anybody else from getting killed," Shannon said. "The last thing we need is a full-scale firefight on our doorstep between the Diamond Seven and Cromwell's men. We'll handle it ourselves. Now, in a few minutes you can go get some dinner. I'll wait here—Kate's volunteered to bring me something to eat after awhile. Meantime, it's getting dark, so let's lock this place down tight—secure the doors and windows, and bar the back door to the jail."

Shannon had just finished lighting the lamps when a loud knock sounded at the office door.

"Who's that?" Shannon called, taking down a shotgun from the rack behind his desk.

"Zeke Webster," a voice cackled. "Got something to show you."

Shannon unlocked the door, and Ezekiel Webster, the town's newspaper editor, walked in.

"Weekly edition," he said, handing Shannon a double sheet of newsprint. "Take a look at that editorial and tell me what you think."

Shannon put down the shotgun and took the paper, and with Cutler and Kate Lipton peering over his shoulder, he read the portion of the paper that Webster had indicated. The headline said OUTRAGE IN CAULDRON COUNTY, and beneath it was a dramatic account of Curt Henderson's death.

"There," Webster said, pointing at a paragraph farther down the page. "That's the best part."

The good people of our county are indebted to our brave sheriff, Clay Shannon, who single-handedly fought his way into the Cromwell ranch today and killed the ringleader of the assassins, a piece of subhuman filth named Wade Stitch, whose removal from the world has undeniably made this planet a far better place to live. Now it only remains for the forces of law and order to do the same for the remainder of the Cromwell vermin, and especially the disgusting criminal who ordered Curt Henderson killed. We refer, of course, to that lowlife scoundrel and bloody-handed murderer, Mr. Archibald Cromwell, a homicidal maniac whose inevitable hanging will complete the good work begun by Sheriff Shannon this morning at the Cromwell ranch.

"How about that?" Webster said gleefully. "That's telling them, eh?"

"You take chances, Mr. Webster," Shannon said. "Arch Cromwell can read too, and he's not going to like this."

"Ah, who cares what he thinks?" Webster chortled. "He wouldn't dare touch me. This is the power of the press in action, son. You stick with me, and we'll get this county cleaned up in no time."

"Just the same," said Shannon, "I'd stay out of dark alleys for a while if I were you."

"Stuff and nonsense," Webster chuckled. "I'm too old to start jumping at shadows. You take care of yourself, son. You're not exactly Cromwell's favorite public servant right now, and he'll be sending people after your scalp."

"They won't get it," Shannon said. "Not without an argument, anyway."

As the evening wore on, Shannon became more and more restless. Randy Cutler had gone to sleep on the old leather couch in the corner, but except for Todd Henderson in his cell in the jail, Shannon was alone in the office. Shannon had asked Kate Lipton to spend the night in the hotel to get her out of harm's way, but she had decided instead to go back to her place over the store to spend the night. Shannon was not happy about this, because he feared that the store might again be a target for an attack by Cromwell's men, but she was adamant.

"I don't like the hotel," she had said. "It's quieter over the store."

"I just hope it stays that way," Shannon muttered, as Kate left the office.

For a while all was indeed quiet, but Shannon was certain that the night would not pass without incident, and events proved him correct. About ten o'clock, the murmur of voices could be heard in the street, a murmur that became an angry rumble as the sound drew nearer. Through the cracks in the shutters, Shannon could see the glint of firelight, and he knew from sad experience what was about to happen. Quickly, he moved over to the bunk and shook his deputy awake.

"Get into the jail," Shannon told him, and lock the door behind you. Take a shotgun with you, and don't let anybody in there except me. Understand?"

Cutler, wide-eyed with apprehension, nodded silently and hurried into the jail, locking the door behind him as Shannon had instructed. Outside, the shouts grew louder, and someone began calling for him to come outside. Shannon checked the cylinder of the Colt and returned the weapon to the holster, leaving the rawhide loop off the hammer. Then he took a deep breath and opened the front door.

There were at least thirty men gathered around the front of the jail. Several of them were holding torches, and the dancing flames cast a fitful orange light over the street as Shannon stepped out onto the walk. All of the men were armed, and Shannon recognized many of the faces from his visit to the Cromwell ranch that morning. Shannon closed the door behind him, locked it, and slipped the key into his pocket.

"Well?" he said.

One heavy-set man wearing two guns tied low moved forward a pace out of the crowd. Shannon recalled that his name was Garth, although whether that was the man's first or last name he could not remember.

"We want Todd Henderson," Garth said. "Either you bring him out or we come in after him."

Shannon hooked his thumbs in his gunbelt and studied the crowd with a practiced eye. He had faced lynch mobs before, and had always been able to talk them into abandoning their purpose. But those had been groups composed mostly of irate but otherwise ordinary citizens, with only a few troublemakers to lead them. This mob was different. Virtually all of them bore the unmistakable marks of experienced gunmen. Cromwell must have sent nearly his entire crew this time, and, looking keenly at them, Shannon could detect no wavering, no doubt, no lack of determination in their truculent faces. These individuals were hired killers, hardcases being paid to do a job, and they would not be influenced by flowery rhetoric or deterred by appeals to non-existent consciences. Still, Shannon knew he had to try.

"Where's Cromwell?" he asked Garth with an ironic smile. "Looks like he stayed home while he sent you boys to do his dirty work for him."

"Never mind where Cromwell is," Garth replied. "We want Todd Henderson, and we want him right now. No arguments, Shannon, no delay tactics while you send for help, no fancy speeches. Just bring that gun-happy little woman-killer out here."

"All right," Shannon said. "No speeches. We'll get right down to business."

He drew the Colt and shot Garth squarely in the left knee.

Garth screamed and went down in a heap, holding his shattered kneecap. Exclamations of dismay filled the street, as the rest of the mob, astonished by this sudden and violent reaction on Shannon's part, fell back a few steps, uncertain as to what to do.

Shannon knew that this was the critical moment. The mob had expected talk, not gunfire. He had caught them by surprise, but the odds against him were still appalling. Would shock and fear prevent these men from opening fire on him, or had he, by shooting Garth, signed his own death warrant?

He cocked the Colt again.

"Five left in the cylinder," he said with a cheerful smile. "Who's next?"

Garth was still squealing in pain.

"Get me outta here!" he wailed. "I'm dyin'."

"No, you're not," Shannon said. "But the next man will be. Come on, boys, any volunteers?"

"Aw, forget this," someone said. "That law dog's crazy. Look at him—he's grinning."

"I'll say he's crazy," said someone else. "He plugged Stitch this morning just as cool as you please, and now he's shot Garth—crippled him for life, most likely. Let's get out of here before he does the same to somebody else."

"Yeah, come on, boys," said a third man as he started to push his way back out of the crowd. "I ain't gettin' paid enough to risk walkin' on sticks for the rest of my life. We'll get Henderson later."

Two men grabbed Garth by the arms and dragged him away as he moaned in pain.

In sixty seconds, the street was dark and empty. Except for the bloodstain in the dust where Garth had fallen, there was nothing to show that anything had occurred.

Shannon holstered the Colt, unlocked the door, and went back inside. He closed the door behind him, relocked it, and leaned against it, waiting for his pulse to slow and his breathing to return to normal.

Twice that day, he had looked into the face of death, and won. And he knew that he had won for just one reason—he had faced the enemy with an appearance of unflinching confidence. This aura of arrogant invincibility had, as it always did, somehow communicated itself to his adversaries, and had made them uneasy. For those few moments they had feared him, and because they feared him, they had hesitated at the critical moment when life and death hung in the balance.

It's a good thing, Shannon told himself, *that those nitwits didn't know how scared I really was.*

Chapter Twelve
The Triumph of Evil

The next day Shannon remained in the office, fearing some further attempt by either Cromwell's men or the Diamond Seven to gain access to Todd Henderson. Kate Lipton had voluntarily assumed the duty of bringing meals to the office for Shannon, Randy Cutler, and Henderson. Still uneasy about Kate's safety, Shannon had argued that the young boy who swept out the jail each day could perform this duty, but did not protest too hard because he found himself looking forward to Kate's visits and to the opportunity to spend time with her.

Shannon had requested that a U.S. Marshal come to Cauldron City to take custody of Todd Henderson, and a telegram that morning had confirmed the marshal's scheduled arrival the following Friday.

"The sooner the better," Randy Cutler said. "I feel like we're sitting on a powder keg here, waiting for somebody to light the fuse."

"I think the fuse is already lit," Shannon replied. "It's just a question of when the keg will explode."

Despite Shannon's apprehensions, the day passed without incident. Kate Lipton brought supper just at dusk, and she and Randy Cutler sat with Shannon at his desk, enjoying the meal. Shannon was attacking his third helping of fried chicken when someone came racing along the boardwalk and began pounding feverishly on the office door. He opened the door and found himself confronted by the town's bootmaker, whose store was some distance up the main street.

"Sheriff!" the man cried. "Come quick! They're wrecking the newspaper office!"

"Who is?"

"Arch Cromwell's men! They've got Zeke Webster, and I'm afraid they're going to beat him to death!"

"Randy, stay here with Kate," Shannon said, striding toward the front door of the office. "Lock up behind me, and don't let anyone in."

"I'm coming too," Kate said.

"Then get the doctor and bring him along," Shannon said. "If what the bootmaker said is right, Webster may be badly hurt."

He raced up the street, torn between worrying about

leaving Randy alone in the jail and fearing for the safety of the old newspaper editor. *I was right,* Shannon thought. *Cromwell can read.*

As he drew near the newspaper office, he saw that a small crowd had gathered in the street in front of it, merely watching rather than doing any harm. But as Shannon approached, he could hear crashing sounds from within the newspaper office, and a splintered chair came flying out of the open door. Both windows of the office had been knocked out, and several other pieces of broken furniture and equipment lay on the sidewalk and in the street.

Two men were lounging in the newspaper's doorway, watching whatever was going on inside. As Shannon crossed the boardwalk, they wheeled about and tried to block his way. Without slackening his pace, Shannon drove his shoulder into the first man's midsection, hurling him back in a heap against the wall. Shannon then rammed a straight left into the face of the second man who now was trying to grapple with him. The man staggered back through the doorway and fell full length on his back on the glass-littered floor of the office. Shannon charged through the doorway, planting one foot in the middle of the fallen man's chest as he passed over him.

Some of the lamps in the office had been broken, but a few were still burning, and by their light Shannon saw two men, one with an axe and the other with a sledge hammer, engaged in beating the newspaper's old printing press into a pile of twisted junk. They were so absorbed in the noisy destruction that they had not noticed Shannon's precipitate arrival. Shannon picked up a handy chair and slammed it against the back of the axe-wielder. The unfortunate man tumbled forward directly into the path of the hammer blow just then being delivered by the second man against the printing press. The recipient of the blow sprawled unconscious across the wrecked press as the man with the hammer stared down at his unintended victim in astonishment. Then he looked up at Shannon and his face darkened with wrath. He started to swing the hammer at Shannon.

"Don't try it," Shannon said. "If you come at me with that thing, I'll have to shoot you, and I'd rather not do that. So just lay the hammer down on the floor, like a good little boy."

But instead of dropping the heavy hammer to the floor as Shannon had warned, the man swung the sledge back over his head and leaped at Shannon, trying to deliver a crushing blow to the lawman's skull.

Shannon shot him dead. The heavy bullet knocked him over onto his back amid the debris on the floor.

The back door of the newspaper office opened abruptly and a third man stuck his head through the doorway. He goggled at the fallen men and at Shannon, who was still standing there with his smoking six-gun in his hand. Beyond the doorway, in the alley behind the newspaper, Shannon could see two more men holding Ezekiel Webster by each arm while still another man was delivering blow after blow to the old man's face, chest, and stomach. Shannon took three quick steps forward and swung the barrel of his six-gun hard against the temple of the man in the doorway. The man bounced off the doorframe into the alley and lay still. Shannon lunged through the doorway and delivered another blow with the six-gun barrel to the back of the head of the man who was hitting Webster. The man crumpled into a heap in the dust. The two men holding Webster's arms immediately let go of him and ran away down the alley as fast as they could go, leaving Webster to fall heavily to the ground. As he fell, his head struck the hard dirt of the alley with a sickening thud.

Shannon put one arm under Webster's shoulders and lifted his head off the ground. Webster's face was bruised and battered, his features covered in blood. One eye was swollen shut, and he was moaning piteously.

"Mr. Webster!" Shannon said. "It's the sheriff. The men who were beating you are gone. You're safe now."

Webster opened his good eye. "Hurts," he said, and slumped back unconscious.

Kate Lipton and the doctor came through the shattered newspaper office and joined him in the alley.

"Let me at him," Doctor Evans said, elbowing Shannon aside. "Miss Lipton, get a lamp and bring it out here, will you?"

"How bad is it?" Shannon asked.

"Bad enough," Evans snapped. "The old fool, he should have known Cromwell wouldn't take that stupid editorial lying down."

Kate Lipton brought the lantern into the alley and held it over Evans' shoulder as the doctor set to work on the injured editor. Shannon went back into the office to check on the opponents he had disposed of on his way through. Only the man who had been hit with the hammer and the hammer-wielder that Shannon had shot remained. The one who had been at the back door and the two men who had been guarding the front were gone.

Shannon checked the man who had been hit with the hammer and saw that he was dead. The gunshot victim was still alive, but Shannon's bullet had hit him low in the chest—it was clear he did not have long to live.

Shannon lifted the man off the floor and laid him on a table near the front of the office, then leaned over the outstretched form.

"Can you hear me?" he said in a loud voice.

"I . . . hear . . . you . . ." the man whispered.

"Who sent you?" Shannon said.

"What . . . ?"

"Who told you to do this?"

"Am I gonna . . . die?" the man asked feebly.

"Yes," Shannon said. "You're going to die. Who told you to wreck the newspaper and beat up Webster? Who gave the orders?"

"He . . . was really . . . mad," the man said. "Went crazy when he saw . . . that thing in the paper . . ."

"Who?" Shannon. "Who went crazy when he saw the paper?"

"Cromwell, o' course," the man wheezed.

"So it was Cromwell who ordered you to wreck the office and beat up the editor?"

"Yeah. He was really mad. Never saw anybody that mad before."

The dying man started to laugh, but the laugh became a cough and ended abruptly in a horrible rattling sound that made Shannon shudder.

Kate Lipton had come back into the office and was standing behind Shannon.

"Did you hear what he said?" Shannon asked.

"Yes," Kate said. "But we knew it anyway, didn't we?"

"Certainly," said Shannon. "But now we have what I've been hoping for—the evidence I need to arrest Cromwell, the evidence admissible in a court of law that I didn't have until just this moment."

"But what that man said before he died doesn't tie Cromwell to Mr. Henderson's murder," Kate protested.

"No," Shannon said, "but at least it will put him in a jail cell, and that's a start."

Shannon became aware that people were now standing on the boardwalk, peering into the newspaper office through the broken windows. He walked out through the door and surveyed the crowd with contempt.

"You people," he said. "You watched this happen,

and not one of you—not one—went to the aid of that old man who was getting beaten up."

"Wasn't our business," said one person. "Nothing to do with us."

"It had everything to do with you," Shannon roared. "This is your town, but you've let it be taken over and terrorized by a bunch of hoodlums because none of you have the courage to stand up to them. But Webster did. He stood up to them, and not just for himself, either. He did it for you. For all of you. And you just stood there and watched while he was beaten senseless. *You all make me sick.* Now get out of here. Go home. Hide there and be glad there are people like Webster and Curt Henderson and Miss Lipton, here, who are willing to stand up for what's right. Go home, all of you, and don't come out again until you're braver than the rats you're sharing your holes with."

The crowd dispersed slowly, with many shocked faces glancing back at Shannon as he stood there on the boardwalk.

"That was quite a speech," Kate Lipton said, taking Shannon's arm and squeezing it tightly. "I never heard you say that many words at one time before."

"I'm sorry I lost my temper," Shannon said. "but those people reminded me of something I read when I was studying for the law."

"What's that?" Kate asked, resting her head on his shoulder.

"If I recall correctly," Shannon replied, "a very wise

man named Edmund Burke said nearly a century ago that *'That only thing necessary for the triumph of evil is for good men to do nothing.'* "

Shannon found Arch Cromwell sitting at a table in the hotel dining room, eating supper. Several other tables in the room were occupied, and the diners looked up curiously as Shannon came through the door.

"Cromwell," Shannon said, "you're under arrest."

Cromwell paused with a fork full of food halfway to his mouth.

"Arrest?" he said. "For what?"

"What difference does it make?" Shannon said. "You're going to jail, whatever it's for."

Cromwell's eyes grew wide. He threw the fork down and started to rise from the table. As he did, his right hand started toward his inside pocket. Shannon grabbed his arm and twisted him around, bending him over double as the derringer for which he was reaching fell harmlessly to the floor.

As Shannon grappled with him, Cromwell struggled furiously, knocking the table over and scattering food, plates, and silverware over the dining room floor. Shannon pulled Cromwell's arms behind his back, then produced a pair of handcuffs from his belt and clamped them on Cromwell's wrists. Cromwell began to shout for help, but Shannon ignored his pleas and propelled him out of the hotel and down the street toward the sheriff's office. As Cromwell stumbled along in

Shannon's grasp, the rancher began to behave more and more erratically, alternately screaming for help and begging Shannon in a falsetto whine to release him. Passersby stopped to watch the two, marveling at the sight of Cauldron County's second largest ranch owner squirming wildly in the grasp of the law and crying like a baby.

When they eventually reached the sheriff's office, Shannon shoved Cromwell into one of the cells, removed the handcuffs, and stepped back, expecting Cromwell to attack him. Instead the rancher stumbled to the cot, curled up on it in the fetal position, and lay there, gently sobbing. *I could almost feel sorry for him,* Shannon thought. *I probably would, if I hadn't seen Curt Henderson lying in the road with a dozen bullets in him, or looked into Ezekiel Webster's bruised face tonight.* He walked out of the cell and closed the iron-barred door behind him.

"I just want you to take a look at him, Doc," Shannon said. "He was in bad shape when I locked him up last night, but he seems quieter this morning."

Doc Evans followed Shannon through the office and into the jail. Cromwell was sitting on the cot in his cell, his head in his hands. From the cell at the opposite end of the cell block, Todd Henderson was also sitting on his cot, watching Cromwell with hatred burning in his eyes.

"How are you feeling, Arch?" the doctor said as Shannon let him into the cell.

"Get him out of here, Evans," Cromwell said, pointing at Shannon. "Get him out of here, I tell you!"

"Take it easy, Arch," Doctor Evans replied, taking out his stethoscope and applying it to Cromwell's chest. "Heart sounds fine. Tell me about these headaches you've been having."

"They're bad," Cromwell said, again putting his head into his hands. "I never knew what pain was until they started."

"Sheriff," Evans said, "I'd like to examine Mr. Cromwell for a few minutes. Will you excuse us?"

"I'll have to lock you both in the cell," Shannon said. "It might be dangerous for you."

"I'll be all right," Evans said. "Could you hang a couple of blankets up on the bars, so we can have some privacy?"

Shannon glanced at Todd Henderson.

"Of course," he said. "Let me know if there's anything else you need."

Twenty minutes later, Evans called for Shannon to let him out of the cell. They went into the office, and Evans slumped into the chair in front of Shannon's desk.

"I'm no expert, you understand," Evans said slowly, "I'm just a country doctor who's never had any training in this sort of thing. But since we talked last, I've read up a bit, and I think we've already guessed the situation."

"Brain tumor?" Shannon said.

Evans nodded.

"That's my diagnosis."

"What's the prognosis?"

"He'll get worse and worse. And then . . ."

"There's nothing you can do for him?"

"Me? No. Not sure there's anything anybody could do. It seems to be pretty far advanced."

"Then tell me this—do you think that a man with that kind of illness is responsible for his actions?"

"Mentally, morally, or legally?"

"Any of those."

"You'll have to find somebody smarter than I am to answer those questions," Evans said, picking up his medical bag. "Why don't you look in those law books of yours?"

"Doc, what I'm asking you is—should a man in his condition be punished for his crimes?"

"Son," Evans said, starting for the door, "I just don't know."

He paused in the doorway.

"I'll tell you what, though," he said. "Why don't you ask all the people Cromwell's harmed? I'll bet they think he should be punished for what he's done to them. Don't you?"

"Yes," Shannon said. "But are they right?"

Doctor Evans shrugged and closed the door behind him.

Shannon went back into the cell block to find Arch Cromwell lying peacefully on his cot, his arms beneath his head, staring blankly at the ceiling.

"How's the headache?" Shannon asked.

Cromwell turned his head to look at Shannon.

"What headache?" Cromwell asked.

"Never mind," Shannon said. "You want to tell me about Curt Henderson's murder?"

"What about the murder of my sister?" Cromwell retorted.

"I told you before. Todd Henderson will stand trial for that. I want to talk about Curt Henderson, not Todd."

"I don't know anything about all that. Stitch must have done it."

"Stitch did do it. I want to know why you ordered it done."

"You're trying to get me to confess, aren't you?" Cromwell said, swinging his legs over the side of the cot. "You're wasting your time. All you've got me for is busting up old man Webster's newspaper office."

"And busting up old man Webster," Shannon said.

"Well, that's all you're going to get, because I'm not talking."

"You're dying, Cromwell. You know that, don't you?"

"That nonsense about the brain tumor? Evans is full of hot air. I'm fine."

"You're dying," Shannon said. "If you have a conscience, if you have anything to say in your own defense, this is the time."

"You can't keep me here, you know," said

Cromwell, looking back at the ceiling. My people will come for me."

"The last time your people came for someone, they went home with their tails between their legs," Shannon said. "I wouldn't count on them too much if I were you."

Cromwell leaped off the cot, seized the tin water cup which hung on the bars, and hurled it at Shannon with all his strength.

"I'll kill you, Shannon!" he screamed. "I'll kill you if it's the last thing I do."

He seized the cell bars and began tearing at them.

"Let me out!" he howled. "Let me out!"

Shannon left him there, babbling incoherently.

Chapter Thirteen
Tragedy

The day passed without incident, and Shannon continued to hope that the worst was over despite his fear that it was not. In the afternoon he sent Randy down to the Henderson store to check on Kate Lipton. An hour later the deputy returned and reported that she had reopened the store and that it was crowded with customers.

"Did you tell her what I said about not coming around to the jail for a while?"

"Yeah," Cutler said. "She wasn't very thrilled about that, but she understands. She knows you want to keep her away from here because you're worried about her safety."

"I'm worried about her safety in that store too," Shannon said. "I wish she'd go to the hotel like I asked her to."

"I think she'll be okay," said Cutler. "Sarah was there, so Miss Lipton isn't alone."

"No wonder you were gone such a long time," Shannon said with a smile.

"I'd like to take Sarah down to the café for some dinner after awhile," Cutler said, "if that's okay with you."

"Certainly," Shannon said.

"I could bring you back a steak," Cutler suggested.

"No thanks," Shannon replied. "That café's steaks are as tough as saddle leather. Just make it a piece of apple pie."

Darkness fell, and now Shannon was on full alert. If there was to be trouble, the hour for it was fast approaching. Suddenly, Randy Cutler burst through the office door, wild-eyed and shaking, and Shannon knew that the hour had arrived.

"The store's on fire!" he cried. "Sarah and I were coming back from the café and we saw the smoke!"

"Where's Kate?"

"I don't know. She was in the store when we left."

"Get the fire brigade," Shannon ordered, heading for the door.

"It's on the way," Cutler replied, starting to run after him.

"Stay here," Shannon said. "Guard the jail."

"But I want to help," Randy lamented.

"Stay here!" Shannon shouted over his shoulder as crossed the boardwalk.

As he entered the street, the town's volunteer fire

brigade came hurtling by. The engine was a new steam pumper, and the boiler's smokestack was spitting sparks as the engine bounced along behind the half-terrified horses that pulled it. Shannon grabbed one of the handrails as the engine came past him and swung aboard, holding on for dear life as the pumper careened around the next corner, headed for the store. Shannon could see ahead of them the pall of smoke hanging over the building, and the glare of flames through the windows. A crowd had already gathered, and several people were filling buckets at the nearby water trough and emptying them against the walls of the store. Shannon searched the crowd for any sign of Kate Lipton, but could not find her.

The fireman driving the steam pumper reined in the horses and brought the machine to a skidding halt in front of the store. As the firefighters piled off and began to unroll the hose, Shannon ran across the boardwalk toward the front door. One of the windows was broken out, and looking through the empty frame he could see that the entire first floor was well alight. Abruptly, the other window, its glass overheated by the fire, cracked and then collapsed, showering broken glass on the walk. Even through the billowing smoke, Shannon could detect the unmistakable odor of kerosene.

As he retreated from the flames that were now licking out of the broken windows, Shannon saw that Sarah Henderson was standing across the street from the store. He hurried over to her.

"Where's Kate?" he said.

"I don't know," Sarah answered, gesturing helplessly at the store. "She was in there when Randy and I left for supper."

"Has anybody seen Miss Lipton?" Shannon called to the crowd.

"She was inside a few minutes ago," someone replied. "I saw her locking up as I came by."

Shannon ran back across the street toward the front door of the burning store.

"Don't go in there, Sheriff!" the fire chief cried. "We'll have the pumper working in a minute!"

Shannon kicked the front door open and rushed inside. Through the leaping flames he could see, at the far end of the room, the stairway to the second floor. The stairs were on fire.

"Kate!" Shannon called. "Kate, where are you?"

There was no reply.

Dodging between the patches of flame, Shannon started up the stairs. As he ascended the burning steps, the heat became more intense, and for a moment he thought that he would not be able to make it to the top. He burst through the doorway at the head of the stairs and into the smoke-filled second floor.

Gagging in the thick smoke, Shannon dropped to the floor and began to crawl through the rooms, shouting for Kate. Just as he was about to give up hope, he heard her voice.

"Here, Clay!" she called. "In the back. Hurry!"

Shannon leaped up and opened the door to the back room, dived through, and then yanked the door shut behind him. The smoke was not as thick in here, and he immediately saw Kate Lipton crouched low in one corner of the room. She was coughing badly in the smoke, but seemed otherwise unharmed.

"We'll never get back down the stairs." Shannon said. "We'll have to go out through the window."

"I tried that," Kate said. "The window won't open."

Shannon yanked at the window, but it was stuck fast, and he was in no mood to waste time trying to unstick it. He picked up a chair and hurled it through the glass, then wrenched a leg off a nearby table and used it to knock out the jagged shards that remained around the edges. He looked out the now-empty sash and saw that the roof of the storage shed was just a few feet below the level of the windowsill.

"Here," he said to Kate, "climb through and then take my hand. I'll lower you down onto the top of the shed."

"What about you?"

"I'll be right behind you. Come on—we've no time to lose."

The smoke was now billowing up through the floorboards, and in the cracks between the boards Shannon could see flames licking up from below. Quickly he helped Kate through the open window and then, holding her hands tightly, leaned out and lowered her down to the safety of the shed roof.

"Now jump," he called. "Hurry."

Kate Lipton slid off the shed roof onto the ground.

"Are you all right?" Shannon called to her.

"Yes. Come on."

Shannon swung his body out of the window, clasped the windowsill tightly, and dropped to the roof of the shed. He tried to land upright but lost his footing on the incline of the roof and half-rolled, half-fell to the ground.

Scrambling up, he took Kate's arm and together they ran along the rear of the store and up the small alley that led from the back of the building to the street.

As they came out into the street, Shannon saw that the crowd had grown and that the fire brigade was pumping water madly through the store's broken windows into the burning first floor.

"It's no good," one of the firemen shouted. "We can't hold it. We don't have enough water pressure to reach the second floor."

The entire front of the building was now a sheet of flames, and Shannon saw that it was only a matter of time before the entire structure collapsed.

"Better get your people back, Chief," he said. "That wall's going to go in a minute."

Reluctantly, the fire chief ordered his men to back away from the burning store, and then directed the fire engine to move off down the street to safety.

"Oh, Clay," Kate Lipton said. "All our work, all those nice things Mr. Henderson brought in to stock the store—everything's gone."

"What happened?" Shannon said. "Did you see who did it?"

"No, I was upstairs. I heard breaking glass, and started to come down into the store to see what had made the noise. Then I smelled kerosene, and when I opened the door at the top of the steps and looked down, the whole store was already in flames. I had to close the door again and run to the back to get away from the smoke."

"I was afraid of something like this," Shannon said with disgust, "but I really didn't think they'd do it, knowing that we could do the same to their store in retaliation. They must not care about that, but why not? They have just as much to lose as we do, unless . . ."

"Unless what?" Kate asked.

Fear knifed through Shannon.

"Unless it was to decoy me out of the jail," he whispered. "Of course, that must be it. They knew I'd come to the store when the fire was reported. It's the same trick they used when they attacked the Taylors. It was a trap, and I fell for it."

He turned and ran back up the street toward the jail.

"Wait for me!" Kate cried. She hurried after him, with Sarah Henderson close behind.

As soon as Shannon rounded the corner and started up the main street toward the sheriff's office, he knew that something was wrong. The front door of the office was off its hinges, lying flat on the sidewalk, and papers were scattered across the walk. Six-gun in hand,

Shannon rushed inside and found Randy Cutler sprawled on the floor, bleeding from a wound in his left leg.

"In there!" Randy said, pointing toward the jail.

The door to the jail was open, hanging by only one hinge. There were buckshot holes in the door, and the direction of the splintering showed that someone had fired through the door from inside the jail. The ring holding the cell keys was missing from its hook beside the door.

Shannon went into the cell block, knowing what he would find. Cromwell's cell door was open, and so was Todd Henderson's. Neither man was anywhere to be seen.

Shannon went back into the office and knelt down beside Randy Cutler.

"What happened?" he asked.

"I locked myself in the jail, like you told me to," Randy said. "They broke in the front door and then started to work on the door to the jail. I warned them to get away, and when they didn't, I fired through the door. Then someone from outside the jail shot through the bars of one of the windows and hit me in the leg. When I went down, they broke the door and charged in. They kicked me in the ribs a couple of times and then unlocked the cells."

Was it Cromwell's men or Diamond Seven?"

"Cromwell's men. They let Cromwell out, then dragged Todd out with them. He was fighting them, but there were too many. They all went out the back door, and I started crawling toward the front, trying to get out to the street to get help. Then you came."

"Any idea where they took Todd?"

"No. But I think they were on foot—I didn't hear any horses galloping away before I started for the front door."

"Let's have a look at that leg," Shannon said. "Hmm—the bullet went straight through, so it must have missed the bone."

He took a clean neckerchief from a desk drawer and tied it tightly to the wound.

"That should hold you until we can get you to the doctor," he told Cutler.

Kate Lipton and Sarah Henderson came in, breathless from running.

"Oh, Randy," Sarah cried, going to her knees and throwing her arms around the young deputy. "Are you badly hurt?"

"I'm okay," Randy mumbled, embarrassed.

"He's not okay," Shannon said. "Somebody get Doc Evans. I'm going to have a look out back."

As Shannon started into the jail, he felt that he was moving through some sort of bad dream. Everything was going wrong—everything. The store was burned, Cromwell had escaped, Randy Cutler was hurt, and Todd Henderson was missing. Once again, Shannon realized, he had failed, failed to fulfill his obligations to the people he was sworn to protect. Before coming to

Cauldron County, he had always enjoyed success as a lawman. Since coming there, he seemed to have had nothing but abject failure.

But the worst was yet to come.

He slipped cautiously out the back door, revolver in hand, to look for tracks or other clues as to the identity and departure route of the people who had broken into the jail.

He had taken only a couple of steps before he saw it.

Between the rear of the jail and the little stable where the horses were kept, a large tree had been left growing between the buildings. In the dim light, Shannon could see that something was dangling from one of the tree's branches. As he drew closer, he saw the limp figure of a man, realizing a split-second later it was Todd Henderson. Cromwell's men had put a rope around his neck, thrown the rope over a tree limb, and hanged him. His body was twisting slowly back and forth at the end of the rope, like some obscene ornament suspended from the branch of the tree.

Shannon remained frozen there for a moment, shocked by the horror of the scene.

In the doorway behind him, Sarah Henderson began to scream.

Chapter Fourteen
The Nightmare

Although Shannon's mind was reeling from the monstrousness of what he had just seen, he knew that he had to gather his wits and concentrate on doing the things that now had to be done. First he cut Todd Henderson's body down and gently laid it out on the ground beneath the tree. Then he went back into the office, helped Randy Cutler up from the floor, and stretched him out on the bunk.

"Miss Lipton's gone for the Doc," Randy said, wincing in pain as Shannon straightened his leg. "What's going on out back? And why is Sarah crying like that?"

Shannon told him about Todd Henderson. His eyes wide with shock, Randy tried to get to his feet.

"I've got to help Sarah," he said. "Let me up—I can walk."

"Just lie still," Shannon told him. "I'll take care of Sarah."

He went back into the jail. Sarah was still by the back door, lying in a heap on the floor and sobbing uncontrollably as she stared out the doorway at her brother's body sprawled on the ground beneath the tree. Shannon closed the door to shut off her view of the corpse.

"Come on, Sarah," Shannon said, "let's go into the office where you can sit down."

"Get away from me!" Sarah shrieked, pulling out of Shannon's grasp and running back through the jail. She stumbled into the office and collapsed beside the bunk where Randy Cutler was lying.

Kate Lipton came in with the doctor, and they both listened in shocked disbelief as Shannon told them of Todd Henderson's fate.

"You sure he's dead?" the doctor asked.

"Yes," Shannon said. He did not go into detail, for Sarah's sake.

"Then I'd better take a look at Cutler," said the doctor, pulling a chair over beside the bunk.

"Where are you going, Kate?" Shannon inquired as Kate started for the jail door.

"To see about Todd," she said.

"Have you ever seen a man who's been hanged?" Shannon asked her.

"No—no, I haven't," she replied, puzzled by the question.

"Then don't go out there," Shannon said. "Believe me, you don't want to see it. Stay here and help Sarah."

Kate sat down on the floor by the bunk next to Sarah Henderson, and began to try to comfort her, but the hysterical sobs continued unabated.

Shannon's mind was functioning more clearly now. The shock that had paralyzed him for the past few minutes had given way to rage, and with the rage came a granite-hard resolve. He drew his Colt six-gun and inspected the cylinder to see that it was fully loaded. Next, he removed a second revolver from a cabinet and checked to make certain that it was also loaded, then shoved it into his belt.

"Where are you going?" Kate asked, her voice barely audible over Sarah Henderson's sobbing.

"After them," Shannon said. "Arch Cromwell is a dead man. He doesn't know it yet, but he's a walking dead man."

"Do you know where he is?" Cutler asked.

"No," Shannon said, "but it doesn't matter. There's not a hole on this earth deep enough to hide him. I'll find him."

"I know where he is, son," said a voice from the doorway. Ezekiel Webster was standing there, leaning on a cane. His face was bandaged so that only one eye and one side of his mouth were visible, but the eye was bright with emotion and his mouth was twisted into a crooked smile. "He's in the Cattleman's Rest Saloon. Since you closed the Silver Spur, the Cromwell crowd's been hanging out there. When Cromwell's men busted him out of jail, that's where they took him, and they've in there now—celebrating, I guess. Is it true that they strung up Todd Henderson?"

"It's true," Shannon said, sliding the second revolver into his waistband.

"You going after them?" Webster asked.

"Naturally."

"Better wait a bit," Webster said. "Cromwell's got a lot of men with him in that saloon, and you'd probably make them very happy by barging in there alone."

"I'll come with you," Randy said.

"No, you won't," Shannon snapped. "Doc, you keep him on that bunk until I come back. I mean it. Zeke, you'd better stay here too. If they find you on the street, they'll might try to finish what they started to do to you the other night."

"Clay," Kate protested, "if Cromwell really is in the Cattleman's Rest, his men aren't going to let you walk out of there with him. They'll kill you."

"Maybe they will," Shannon said heavily, "but I'm going. It's the least I can do for the Hendersons and for the people of this town. I still carry the star, Kate, and right now that star is tarnished—badly tarnished. I'm going to make it bright again."

"How?" Kate cried. "By getting holes shot in it?"

"No," Shannon replied. "By putting Cromwell where he belongs—in a pine box. No more cat and mouse, no more legal hocus-pocus, no more worrying about evidence or punishing a sick man. Cromwell's dead. Period."

"I want to come too," Randy Cutler said, trying to get to his feet. "I'm your deputy."

Shannon walked out, sending the door crashing shut behind him.

One quick glance through the window of the Cattleman's Rest Saloon revealed five men gathered in a circle around the bar. Shannon recognized all of them as Cromwell's hired gunmen. Arch Cromwell was in the middle of the circle, raising his glass in a toast. Several other men were sitting at the tables, watching the celebration. Shannon did not recognize any of them, and he hoped that they were just casual visitors to the saloon and not more of Cromwell's gunhands.

Five against me for sure, Shannon thought, *plus Cromwell himself. More, if the people at the tables interfere or other Cromwell men come into the saloon.*

He debated briefly whether to go around to the back door and enter there, but no one at the bar was paying any attention to the front doors, so he decided to go in that way instead. He picked up a chair that was sitting on the covered boardwalk outside the saloon and heaved it through one of the saloon's large windows. As the startled crowd turned to look at the broken window, Shannon came through the swinging doors, the Colt cocked and ready.

"Everybody freeze!" Shannon bellowed. "First man

who moves gets a .45 bullet in the belly. You, Cromwell, put down that glass and come over here. Keep your hands where I can see them—I haven't forgotten that derringer you carry."

Cromwell laughed.

"You've made several mistakes tonight, Shannon," he said, "but this one's your last. Take him, boys."

The five Cromwell men spread out, hands hovering over their holsters, watching for their chance. It came quickly, as another Cromwell gunman burst through the swinging doors behind Shannon, holding a pistol which he was in the process of pointing at Shannon's head. Shannon twisted his body around and fired, knocking the newcomer off his feet. In this brief moment of Shannon's distraction, the rest of the Cromwell men went for their guns.

Shannon fired twice in quick succession. Two men fell to the floor, but meanwhile the three remaining gunmen had cleared leather and were starting to shoot at Shannon. Bullets whipped past him, plucking at his clothing. One slug seared his left side, and another burned along his left forearm. Shannon dropped another of his adversaries with one more quick shot. The two surviving Cromwell men were still shooting, and one of their bullets gouged the outside of Shannon's left thigh, almost causing him to fall, but he remained on his feet. At that moment another pair of gunmen came bursting through the swinging doors, six-guns in their hands. Shannon killed one of them before he could pull the trigger, but the second got off a quick shot at Shannon. The bullet scorched Shannon's cheek, and with the last cartridge in the Colt he downed the man who had fired it.

With the Colt now empty, Shannon drew the second revolver from his belt. As he did so, the back door of the saloon crashed open, and a man came running through carrying a shotgun. Shannon fired at him and he collapsed, dropping the shotgun.

When the gunfight began, Cromwell had jumped over the bar and hidden behind it. Shannon now saw him breaking for the back door, and sent two hasty shots after him. Cromwell stumbled and cried out as one of the slugs grazed his arm, but he remained on his feet and dived out the door.

In desperation, for he knew that he was running out of time, Shannon whirled back toward the two remaining Cromwell men. *Two left,* he thought, raising the six-gun. *I've been lucky so far, but even these incompetent clods can't keep missing me forever.*

But with their boss running away and Shannon cocking his revolver to fire at them again, Cromwell's two surviving employees hastily decided that they did not want to join their dead comrades on the floor. They dropped their guns and raised their hands, protesting that they had surrendered. Shannon found himself, still alive, confronting two very frightened men with their hands held high above their heads, the fight suddenly gone out of them.

The people who had been sitting at the tables had

dived for cover when the shooting began, and, fortunately for Shannon, none of them had joined in the gunfight. Shannon covered them with his half-empty revolver.

"Any of you want in on this?" he asked in an encouraging tone.

"Not me," one man said, rising slowly from behind an overturned table. "I'm a stranger in town. I just came here in for a drink. I'll leave now, if that's okay with you, Sheriff."

Several others nodded in agreement.

"Yeah, this isn't our fight," one said.

"All right, then, move out," Shannon said.

As the shaken spectators headed rapidly for the back door, Shannon again turned his attention to the two Cromwell gunmen who were left standing. He wanted to haul them off to jail, for he knew that they were hired gunmen who probably had Henderson blood on their hands, but his first priority had to be Cromwell, and Cromwell was at that very moment escaping into the dark. Shannon realized with disgust that he would either have to kill the two men or let them go, for he was alone and there was no time to take prisoners.

"Get out of here," he said to the two Cromwell men. "Get out of town, out of the county, out of the territory. If I ever see you again, I'll shoot you on sight."

They ran from the saloon without looking back. A moment later, horses could be heard galloping away from the saloon. The sound faded quickly and was gone.

Shannon leaned against one of the tables, trying to get his breath and marveling that he was still alive.

How did I live through all that? he wondered. *How could so many men have missed me so many times at such close range?* He knew that it had happened before in many frontier gunfights, some of them famous, when men under extreme stress had failed repeatedly to hit their targets at point-blank range. Due to good luck or bad marksmanship, Shannon had just survived a similar experience. Exhilaration flooded through him as he felt the euphoria of a man who has been given a totally unexpected second chance to live.

His elation was short-lived, however, for at that moment the world came crashing down around him.

"Hey, Sheriff," called one of the men who had started to leave. "This guy you shot over here by the back door is in a bad way."

"So what?" Shannon said coldly.

"Well, I just thought you might be interested," the man said. "He's wearing a badge."

Shannon's heart nearly stopped beating.

"What?" he said. "Who is it?"

"I dunno," the man replied. "Like I told you, I'm a stranger in town."

Hardly daring to breathe, Shannon ran over to the back door, looked down, and nearly choked on his own bile. The man on the floor was Randy Cutler.

As if in a horrible dream, Shannon saw the bullet hole in Cutler's chest and the deputy's contorted, ashen face, images that would be burned in Shannon's soul forever.

"I told you to stay in the office," Shannon cried, kneeling beside the injured deputy. "For the love of heaven, man, why did you come charging in here like that? I thought you were one of them."

"Had . . . to . . . help . . ." Cutler said.

He reached up with his hand and touched the deputy's badge on his chest.

"Star," he said. "Carry . . . star . . . like you."

His eyes closed, and his body went limp. His breathing, which had been growing more labored, now stopped altogether.

"No!" Shannon shouted. "NO! NO! NO!"

"Can you believe that?" someone said. "The sheriff killed his own deputy."

Half-mad with grief and guilt, Shannon jumped up, brandishing his revolver and screaming for everyone to leave the saloon. The spectators scattered like rabbits out the two doors, leaving Shannon alone with his fallen friend. He went again to his knees, cradling Randy's head in his arms.

"I'm sorry, Randy," he whispered. "I didn't know it was you. I'm so sorry."

Doctor Evans came into the saloon, looked around in disbelief at the carnage, then rushed over to the spot where Shannon was kneeling beside his deputy.

Evans felt Cutler's throat for a pulse and found none.

"He's gone," Evans said. "Who shot him?"

"I did," Shannon said.

Doctor Evans' mouth fell open.

"*You* shot him?" Evans said incredulously.

"Yes," Shannon whispered in an agonized voice. "I did it. I killed him."

At that moment, Shannon wanted desperately to die, for he had never known such pain. As the delirium of his despair swept over him, it was as if he were staring down a long, dark tunnel at the one thing left on earth that there was to see—the dead face of a young man who had wanted above all else to be like Clay Shannon and wear a star.

Perhaps the only thing that saved Shannon's sanity in those minutes was the sudden, jarring recollection that amid the chaos and the anguish, Arch Cromwell, the murderous architect of all of this tragedy, had gotten away, and disappeared into the night.

Almost blinded by sorrow and remorse, Shannon leaped up and ran headlong out the back door into the side street. Several men were gathered there, peeping into the saloon.

"Did any of you see Arch Cromwell come out of there?" Shannon demanded.

"Sure," said one of the onlookers. "He come out a minute ago. He was wounded, too. Look."

He pointed to the spots of blood plainly visible in the dry dirt of the street.

Shannon's grief had now turned to fury, and the fury sustained him in this, the darkest moment of his life.

Grimly he began to follow the blood trail, reloading his Colt revolver as he went. A trickle of blood was running down his leg from the place where the bullet had creased his thigh, but he ignored both the blood and the pain.

You might as well stop running, Cromwell, he thought. *No matter where you go, I'll be there, waiting. And I'll make you pay for all of this, Cromwell. I'll make you pay.*

The trail led up the steps of the building that housed Cauldron County's sole vestige of culture, a little theater where traveling performers sometimes appeared and the local repertory company held forth a few nights a month. The theater's double doors were standing wide open, and the blood trail led right through them. People were running out of the theater, and Shannon dimly recalled that a rehearsal for a forthcoming play had been scheduled for that night.

One of the women fleeing the theater seized Shannon's arm.

"A man just ran in there!" she cried. "He was all bloody, like he'd been shot."

Shannon pushed the frightened woman aside and raced up the steps to the open doors.

Inside, the theater was dimly lit by a few oil lamps spaced out around the walls, and some of the footlamps at the front of the stage were also lit. Together, these gave just enough illumination to enable Shannon to see Cromwell run down the aisle and climb the steps to the stage.

"Hold it, Cromwell," Shannon roared. "You can't get away—I've got you cold. Turn around and face me."

Cromwell paused, then wheeled around to look at Shannon. In the glow of the footlamps, Shannon could see that the rancher's eyes were glazed, and that blood was dripping from a flesh wound in his left arm. Suddenly Cromwell's hands went to the sides of his head and he doubled over, moaning.

"Leave me alone!" he cried. "My head hurts!"

"It won't after I blow it off!" Shannon told him.

"Don't kill me," Cromwell begged. "I haven't even got a gun. Please don't kill me. I don't want to die."

"Neither did the people you killed," Shannon said. "And neither did the people I've killed because of you."

He aligned the sights of the Colt squarely on the middle of Cromwell's forehead, and started to squeeze the trigger.

Cromwell was pressing his hands hard against his temples now. Tears were running down his cheeks, and there was agony in his eyes.

"Then do it!" Cromwell screamed. "Go ahead, do it! I don't care! I can't stand this pain in my head anymore! Kill me, Shannon—get it over with! Please! Please!"

Shannon stood there, holding pressure on the trigger, willing himself to fire the shot that would end Cromwell's life. In that moment, he thought of all the evil that this man had done, all the lives he had destroyed, and he hated Cromwell more than he had ever hated any human being before.

But something inside him wouldn't let him pull the trigger. Perhaps it was because Cromwell was unarmed, perhaps it was just because the man was sobbing so pathetically. Or perhaps it was the oath that Shannon had taken to uphold the law simply would not let him kill a man out of naked hatred or a desire for personal revenge.

"You're under arrest, Cromwell," Shannon croaked. "And this time you won't get away. You're going to stand trial for all the foul things you've done."

For a few moments Cromwell remained in his crouched position. Then he slowly straightened up, dropping his arms loosely to his sides. The pain in his eyes faded, and his contorted facial muscles relaxed. Shannon watched this transition with astonishment. It was as if he were witnessing some sort of supernatural metamorphosis from wild-eyed animal back to rational human being. The surreal spectacle sent a chill up Shannon's back.

Cromwell wiped his eyes with his sleeve, and when he spoke again, it was in a perfectly normal voice.

"So you're not going to kill me?" he said calmly. "Ah, yes, I understand. Now that I'm your prisoner, and you *can't* kill me." He began to laugh. "That stupid badge on your chest won't *let* you kill me, will it? You're a fool, Shannon. A naive, law-abiding idiot. I'll hire lawyers, I'll bribe judges, I'll intimidate jurors, and in the end I'll walk out of your stinking courtroom free as air. And when I do, I'll spit in your face as I go through the door. I'll . . ."

Something moved behind Cromwell in the shadows of the darkened stage. Before Shannon could react, an explosion ripped through the theater and the light of twin muzzle flashes momentarily illuminated the scene. In the fleeting glare, Shannon saw that Sarah Henderson was standing ten feet behind Cromwell with a double-barreled shotgun pointed at Cromwell's back. The girl had just fired both barrels through the man's spine.

The double charge of buckshot catapulted Cromwell off the stage and sent him tumbling head over heels into the aisle of the theater. He lay there on the floor, twisted and broken, like a torn rag doll that some child had grown tired of and thrown away.

Sarah Henderson lowered the shotgun and walked forward to the edge of the stage. There was a triumphant gleam in her eyes, and her mouth was curled into a bitter smile.

"That's *my* brand of justice, Sheriff" she hissed. "Now tell me, which is better—mine or yours?"

Shannon stared at her for a long moment, then holstered the Colt, turned, and walked slowly up the aisle of the theater and out into the night.

Chapter Fifteen
Parting

Randy Cutler was laid to rest in a quiet corner of the cemetery that stood on a little hill just outside the town. It was a simple ceremony, presided over by Cauldron County's one and only clergyman. A brief eulogy, a quiet prayer, and the singing of an old, familiar hymn marked the young man's passing from the world that he had lived in for so short a time.

Shannon stood a little way apart from the crowd, listening. He would liked to have been right at the graveside, for it seemed to him that he owed Randy Cutler at least that much. But the hostile stares of the others in attendance at the funeral had made it clear that he was an unwelcome presence, and so he moved away a few yards in order not to disturb the ceremony.

The coffin was lowered into the ground, and as the

dirt was shoveled in on top of it, the spectators turned and moved away, back toward town. Kate Lipton had been standing next to Sarah Henderson, holding her arm during the service. The two women now came toward Shannon, and he saw that while Kate Lipton had been weeping, Sarah Henderson's eyes were dry and hard.

They stopped in front of him, looking at him, Kate Lipton with sympathy, Sarah Henderson with naked hatred.

"I'm sorry, Sarah," Shannon said. "I wish . . ."

Sarah Henderson slapped him across the face as hard as she could.

"My father asked you to help us," she said, "and now my father's dead, and my brother's dead, and the man I wanted to marry is dead—all because of you. And in the end I had to do your job for you, to kill Cromwell because you didn't have the courage to do it yourself."

"That's not fair, Sarah," Kate Lipton protested. "Randy's death was just a horrible accident, and Clay risked his life again and again trying to help us. How can you say such terrible things to him?"

"I'll say what I like to him," Sarah Henderson said, "and what I say to you, Mr. Shannon, is this—*get out of Cauldron County. You're not wanted here.*"

She jerked her arm out of Kate's grasp and walked off.

"I'm sorry, Clay," Kate said. "She's wrong to say what she said, and wrong to feel the way she does."

"That's the worst part of it," Shannon said sadly. "She's not wrong. She's right. I failed to prevent her father's murder, I failed to protect her brother when he was in my custody, and I killed Randy Cutler. By accident, yes, but I killed him just the same."

Kate looked past Shannon to the buckskin horse that stood saddled close behind him, saddlebags and blanket roll in place behind the saddle.

"You're going away?" she asked.

"Yes. Sarah's going to get her wish. I'm leaving Cauldron County."

"But why?" Kate cried. "You brought Cromwell down and killed or drove away his men. Because of you, the county is peaceful and safe again."

"The price was too high," Shannon said. "Much too high."

"The price of peace is always high," Kate replied heatedly. "You have nothing to be ashamed of. Don't go, please. We're going to rebuild the store, and Sarah will forgive you in time. Stay here, Clay. Stay with me."

Shannon shook his head.

"I can't, Kate," he said. "I wish I could, but there are too many ghosts here, ghosts that I can't live with. I'm sorry."

Tears were running down Kate Lipton's cheeks.

"Will you ever come back again?" she asked.

"Perhaps," Shannon said. "Someday."

Kate looked deep into his eyes for a moment, and saw the truth there.

"No," she said. "You'll never come back. And I'll never see you again. Ever."

She wiped her tears away and then reached up and kissed him gently on the lips.

"Good-bye, Clay," she said. "May God be with you, wherever you go."

Then she turned and hurried away down the hill. Shannon watched her go, wondering if she would look back, but she did not.

When everyone had left and he was alone in the cemetery, Shannon walked over to Randy Cutler's grave and stood for a moment looking down at it. A white wooden cross stood at the head of the grave, surrounded by the flowers that Sarah Henderson had left there. Slowly Shannon reached into his pocket and withdrew the badge that he had worn when he was sheriff of Cauldron County. Reaching down, he placed it against the foot of the cross.

Then he mounted the buckskin and sat there in the saddle for a moment, gazing down at the metal star gleaming among the flowers.

Cash Bonham was right, he thought. *It's a long fall. A long, long fall.*

He swung the buckskin's head around and put the horse into a slow trot. It was, he decided, very appropriate that the trail out of Cauldron County led sharply downhill.

PART THREE

THE TOWN TAMER

Chapter Sixteen
Yellow Flats

The town sat in the middle of a sun-baked plain, a collection of unpainted wooden buildings that huddled together in the desert vastness as if seeking comfort from each other. Clay Shannon reined in the buckskin at the town limits to read the weathered sign posted there. *Yellow Flats,* it said. *Population 103.* The signboard bore several bullet holes which made it difficult to read, but it was apparent that the sign had originally read *Population 107.* Someone had slapped a thin coat of paint over the *107* and substituted the present number.

"Looks like some people left," Shannon said to the horse. "One way or another."

He rode slowly down the town's lone street, maneuvering occasionally to avoid the tumbleweeds that were blowing along in the dust. Many of the buildings were empty, with shutters or doors flapping loosely in the wind. The only sign of life on the entire street was a man in a bartender's apron sitting in a chair on the covered boardwalk outside a rickety-looking building that had the words *Green Lantern Saloon* scrawled in bilious green paint across the false front. The man stared at Shannon as he rode by, but Shannon ignored him.

At the far edge of town he found what he was looking for—a building whose sign said simply *Freight Office*. There was a wagon with a broken wheel leaning against the side of the building, and beyond it was a dilapidated board corral occupied by eight listless-looking mules.

Shannon tied the buckskin to the hitchrail in front of the office, then unbuckled one of the saddlebag flaps and extracted from the bag a tattered piece of newspaper. The front door of the freight office was open, and Shannon paused at the entrance, waiting for his eyes to adjust to the dimness of the interior. A man sitting at a desk against the far wall looked up at him without enthusiasm.

"Help you?" he said.

"Looking for Mr. George Porter," Shannon replied.

"I'm George Porter," the man said without rising from the chair. "Who're you?"

Shannon walked over to the desk and laid the newspaper on the desk.

"You advertise for a marshal?" he said.

Porter picked up the piece of newspaper, glanced at

the small advertisement in the lower corner, then shoved the paper back across the desk to Shannon.

"Yeah," he said. "Why?"

"I'm interested in the job," Shannon said.

Porter leaned back in the chair, noting Shannon's dusty clothes and unshaven cheeks.

"Looks like you rode a piece to get here," he said. "You must need a job pretty bad. What's your name?"

Shannon told him.

Porter's eyebrows went up and he leaned forward in the chair.

"I've heard of you," he said. "You were marshaling up in Kansas for a while, weren't you?"

"Yes."

"Yeah, I remember you now," Porter said, standing up and shaking hands with Shannon. "Fastest gun in Kansas, they called you. Helped clean up Longhorn and some of the other trail towns when the Texas herds were coming north. What in the world brings a man with your background to a place like Yellow Flats?"

"Unemployment," Shannon said. "What about the job?"

Porter looked pained.

"I'm sorry, Mr. Shannon," he said, "but you're too late. The position's been filled. I just hired a man a few days ago. I'm afraid you've ridden a long way for nothing."

Shannon rubbed his tired eyes. *Another dead end,* he thought. He rose from the chair.

"Thanks anyway," he said.

"I'm really sorry," said Porter. "Say, you look beat. Is there anything I can do to help?"

"No, thanks," Shannon replied. "I'll just get something to eat and move on. Sorry to have bothered you."

"No bother," Porter said, following Shannon to the door. "Next town is Sand Wells, about fifty miles west. You might try there."

"Thanks," Shannon said. "I might."

Shannon pushed open the swinging doors of the Green Lantern Saloon and entered. Except for the bartender who had been sitting outside earlier, the place was empty. Shannon went to a table in the corner and sat down in the chair that faced the doorway. He was stiff and sore from too many hours in the saddle, and the cool semi-darkness of the saloon was a welcome relief from the midday glare.

The bartender was listlessly polishing shot glasses with a bar towel.

"What'll you have, Mister?" he said.

"Can I get a meal here?" Shannon asked.

"This ain't no restaurant," said the bartender. "I got some coffee in the back room, though, if you want it."

"Coffee, then," Shannon said.

"Haven't seen you in here before," the bartender commented as he put the coffee mug down on the table. "New in town?"

"Just passing through," Shannon said, sipping the

coffee. It was muddy and stale, but he had been riding since dawn and even bad coffee was preferable to none at all.

"Well, watch out, then," the bartender said. "We got a new marshal who thinks he's tough, and he don't like drifters much."

"I'll keep it in mind," Shannon replied.

"You've got a big mouth, Harley," said someone from the doorway. "Get on back behind the bar and keep it shut for a while."

The speaker was a stocky man wearing a badge pinned to his checkered shirt. He pushed the swinging doors aside and walked over to the table where Shannon was sitting.

"Saw you come in," he said. "My name's Paxton. I'm the marshal here in Yellow Flats, and Harley's right—I don't like drifters. Especially ones with tied-down holsters and a hard look, and you got both. Where you headed?"

"West," Shannon said.

"Why?"

Shannon suppressed his rising irritation. In his years as a lawman he had questioned more than one stranger about his intentions, but it was unpleasant to be on the other side of the conversation.

"Looking for a job," he said, finishing the coffee. "Heard they might need a marshal over in Sand Wells."

"You a lawman?" Paxton asked, frowning.

"Was," Shannon replied.

Paxton nodded understandingly.

"Yeah, I know how that is," he said. "I was out of work for a while too before I got this job. Hey, Harley, bring me a beer will you?"

He took off his hat and placed it on the table, his manner more relaxed now. He sat down and extended his hand across the table.

"Fred Paxton," he said. "Sorry about the roust, but I got to be careful. It's pretty tense around here these days."

Shannon shook hands with Paxton and introduced himself.

"What's the trouble here?" Shannon asked.

"Too much meanness and too little law," Paxton said. "This town's a real sinkhole. I wish now I hadn't taken the job, but I was broke and hungry."

"Yes," Shannon said with a crooked smile. "I know how *that* is."

"No use going to Sand Wells, I'm afraid," Paxton continued. "That place is practically a ghost town now. They won't be looking to hire anybody." He shook his head sympathetically. "Things are kinda tough these days for anybody looking for a marshaling job, ain't they? I was lucky to get this one."

Three men came into the saloon, talking in loud tones.

"Whiskey!" one of them, a man with flaming red hair, said to the bartender. "None of that rotgut you been passin' out, either. Gimme a bottle of somethin' decent for a change."

"Only got one kind," the bartender said sulkily. "In this dump, one bottle's about as bad as another."

The red-headed man reached across the bar and grabbed the bartender by the shirt, dragging him halfway across the bar. Then he pulled out his six-gun and shoved the muzzle up against the bartender's forehead.

"I don't want no backtalk from you," the gunman snarled. "You gimme some good whiskey or I'll blow your stupid head off."

"Hey, you!" Paxton said, rising from his chair at Shannon's table. "None of that, now."

He walked over to the man holding the six-gun and stood nose-to-nose with him.

"Put the gun away, cowboy," he said. "If you don't like what they serve here, there's another saloon down the street."

Shannon watched the exchange with growing concern. Paxton had made the cardinal mistake of placing himself between two of the toughs, leaving his back unprotected. Shannon had seen more than one Kansas lawman pay the price for that kind of carelessness.

"Don't push me, Paxton," the red-headed man with the pistol in his hand said. "You been throwin' your weight around a lot since you got here, and I'm tired of it."

Paxton grabbed the man's revolver by the barrel, trying clumsily to wrest it out of his hand. As the two men struggled for possession of the gun, the man standing behind Paxton reached over and yanked the marshal's six-gun out of its holster, cocked it, and fired it into the small of Paxton's back.

As Paxton went down, Shannon came out of his chair, his Colt in hand.

"Hold it!" he shouted. "Put the guns on the bar and back off."

With a curse, the man who had shot the marshal swung the pistol in Shannon's direction. Shannon fired, knocking the shooter hard against the bar. The man slid to the floor and lay still.

"You're next," Shannon said to the red-headed man, who was staring open-mouthed at Shannon.

"Hey, I didn't do nothin'," the man said. "Take it easy!" He hastily put his revolver on the bar, and backed away.

The third man raised his hands and stepped back also.

"You two—unbuckle your gunbelts and drop them on the floor," Shannon said. "Good. Now, turn around and face the bar. First one who moves gets it just the way the marshal did."

After collecting the pistol from the top of the bar, Shannon picked up the gunbelts and tossed them aside. Then he bent over Fred Paxton.

"How bad is it?" the bartender said, coming around the end of the bar to look.

"He's dead," Shannon replied. "So's the man who shot him. You got a jail in this town?"

"Sure," said the bartender.

"Show me."

The bartender led the way to the jail while Shannon herded the two remaining men out the saloon door and down the street to the town marshal's office. Drawn by the sound of gunfire, a small crowd of curious onlookers had gathered around the saloon entrance, and as Shannon came out with the two gunmen, the crowd followed them down the street.

Inside the office, Shannon looked around, found the keys to the jail, and shoved his prisoners into one of the cells. He came back into the office, tossed the keys on the desk, and walked out the door. The bartender was still standing outside, a dazed look on his face.

"Did Paxton have any deputies?" Shannon asked.

"Yeah, one," the bartender replied. "He ain't around much, though."

"Well, you'd better find him and tell him what happened. I'll be at that café down the street if he wants to ask me any questions."

Shannon had just finished his meal when four men entered the café. Three stood waiting by the door while the fourth approached the table. Shannon recognized Porter from the freight office.

"I just came from the saloon," Porter said. "I saw Fred Paxton's body and heard about you jailing the men who killed him. May my associates and I join you?"

When they were seated, Porter looked at Shannon inquiringly.

"Looks like the job you came here for is open now," he said. "You still interested?"

"Maybe," Shannon said. "Something's going on in this town. What is it?"

Porter glanced the other men seated at the table.

"As you may know," he began, "the badlands north of here are a haven for every thief, killer, and renegade in this part of the country. There's no law there, none at all, so it's an ideal place for men on the run, men who need a place to hide until their next job. Lately there's been a whole pack of 'em holed up in that area, an outfit that calls itself the Trench gang, led by a man named Hack Trench. Normally we wouldn't care what they do up there, but lately they've been passing through Yellow Flats on their way in and out of the badlands. When they come, sometimes they hang around here for days, drinking and fighting among themselves and hoorawing the town whenever they feel like it. Women aren't safe on the streets, merchants aren't safe in their stores. A couple of townspeople have been killed, and we're sick of all the violence. The gang's got the whole town scared, and a few residents are pulling out, going somewhere else to find some peace and quiet. My friends and I don't want Yellow Flats to die, Mr. Shannon. We've all got business interests here, and we want Hack Trench and his hoodlums stopped. That's why we advertised for a lawman."

"Tell him about the others," one of Porter's associates said. "He's got a right to know."

"Yeah," Porter said. "We've had three town marshals over six months. One was beaten to death by the toughs, the second was bushwhacked in an alley one night, and of course you saw what happened to Fred Paxton today. Now he's dead too, so we'd like to make you a proposition."

"I hear that Paxton had a deputy," Shannon said. "Why not make him marshal and let him take care of it?"

"You misunderstand me," Porter said. "We've tried to do things legally, and you can see what's it's gotten us. So we don't want another marshal, Mr. Shannon. We want a town tamer, plain and simple, and we'll pay you five hundred dollars to do the job. One hundred up front, the rest when you've cleaned up Yellow Flats so it's safe for people to walk the streets again."

Shannon shook his head. *I'm desperate*, he thought, *but not that desperate—yet.*

"You've got the wrong man, Mr. Porter," he said. "A town tamer is nothing but a hired gun who moves from town to town, taking money for killing whoever his employers say needs killing. I work within the law."

"We'll give you a badge if it will make you feel better," Porter said. "But we don't want these outlaws arrested. We want them run out or wiped out so we can have our town back."

"Sorry," Shannon said. "A killer with a badge is still nothing but a killer."

Porter raised an eyebrow.

"You're a man of high standards, Mr. Shannon," he

said. "Anyone can see that. But at the moment you're unemployed, down on your luck, probably down to your last dollar as well. You may have been a first-class peace officer once, but, if you'll pardon me for saying so, it looks to me that right now you're about out of aces. Tell me, do you think you're going to get any better offers than the one we just made you?"

Shannon hesitated. It was months since he had left Cauldron County, months in which he had drifted from place to place, unable to obtain a marshal's appointment. He was growing more tired, more shabby, and more apprehensive about the future. This town, Yellow Flats, was nothing but a speck on the map, an insignificant little dot in the far reaches of the desert, and a long way from the glory days of Dodge City, Abilene, and Wichita.

But those days were gone now. Now there was only Yellow Flats.

Half hating himself, he made his decision.

"All right, Mr. Porter," he said. "I'll take the job. But only under certain conditions."

"Name them."

"First, I must be the duly appointed Marshal of Yellow Flats. I won't work without a badge."

"Agreed."

"Next, I want you and your associates to understand what you're getting into here. I'm familiar with the situation in the badlands, and I know the kind of people I'll be facing. You're right about one thing—half measures aren't going to get rid of them. You say you're sick of violence, but that's what you're buying here, because only violence will get this job done."

"We know that. That's why we're paying you five times what Fred Paxton was making."

"Furthermore, let me make this clear right at the beginning—I do things my way, with no interference from anyone. This is going to be a tough job, and tough measures will be required. Some of your fellow citizens are going to be unhappy about that. Which brings me to the final condition, and that's this—once I start, I'm left to finish the job. I won't quit on you, and you must agree not to quit on me, by which I mean that you won't try to fire me in the middle of everything just because you don't like my methods. That's the way town tamers work, Mr. Porter. That's what you're buying with your money."

"The job's yours, Mr. Shannon," Porter said. He reached into his coat and removed his wallet. "Here's the hundred in advance. What do you want to do first?"

"First," Shannon said, rubbing his chin, "I want a bath and a shave. After that, we'll see."

Chapter Seventeen
Tough Measures

Shannon had no difficulty obtaining a room at the Yellow Flats Hotel, for there were no other guests. After a much-needed bath, he donned his only clean pair of pants and was standing before the mirror in his room shaving when a knock sounded at the door.

Shannon put down the razor and drew his six-gun.

"Yes?"

"Name's Ferrum," replied a nasal voice. "I'm your deputy."

When Shannon opened the door, Ferrum entered and sprawled himself carelessly across the room's sole chair. He was a short, rat-faced man with a two-day growth of beard and eyes that darted about the room, never meeting Shannon's.

"So you got Paxton's job, eh?" said Ferrum. It was more of a challenge than a question.

"Looks that way," Shannon agreed, resuming shaving while he watched Ferrum in the mirror.

"I should have been given the star," Ferrum said. "I been deputy marshal here for nearly a year, but Porter and his crowd keep hiring other people to be marshal."

Shannon rinsed the razor and put it away.

"From what I've heard, you're lucky they didn't give you the job. Where were you today when Paxton was shot?"

"Around," Ferrum said. "Why?"

"If he'd had some backup, he might still be alive right now."

"I can't nursemaid every two-bit drifter Porter hires," Ferrum mumbled sulkily.

"Why not?" Shannon snapped. "That's your job, Deputy—to back up your marshal or any other lawman who needs help."

"Okay, okay," Ferrum said. "Keep your shirt on. You got the job, and I got left out, as usual. No hard feelings. But take a tip from me—this crummy burg ain't worth dyin' for."

"Then you shouldn't have sworn to defend it," Shannon said.

"You're right there, brother," Ferrum agreed.

Shannon decided not to engage in a debate with Ferrum over the matter.

"There are two prisoners over in the jail," he said. "Does this town have a magistrate?"

"A what? Oh, you mean Judge Billy?"

"Find him. Tell him court's in session."

"Judge Billy" proved to be an elderly man who dispensed justice from a rear table in the town's small and dingy second saloon, which was appropriately named the Rathole. The judge was bleary-eyed and exuded an odor of sweat and alcohol. Shannon watched with disgust as he fined the two participants in Paxton's murder ten dollars each and let them go.

As they mounted their horses, the two ex-prisoners were laughing openly about their unexpected release from the jail. Shannon walked over to hitchrail.

"Don't ever come to Yellow Flats again," he said to them. "The next time I see you, I'll shoot you down in the street. Do you understand me?"

"You're talking pretty tough for somebody who just got a dead man's job," the red-haired man growled.

The Colt appeared in Shannon's hand. "Open your mouth again and I'll shoot you right now," he said.

The two men looked at the gun Shannon was pointing at them, then quickly turned their horses and rode out of town without speaking or looking back.

Shannon went back into the Rathole Saloon where Judge Billy was collecting his judicial fee—a free drink of whiskey from the bar. Shannon walked over to him, grasped him firmly by his coat collar and the shiny seat of his pants, and ran him out the door of the saloon into the street. There he lifted the squirming man off his feet and deposited him into the nearest water trough.

"The next time I bring a prisoner to you," Shannon said to the spluttering jurist, "you'd better be sober, or I'll throw *you* in jail. Any questions, Your Honor?"

"Now, see here, young man," Judge Billy cried, still sitting in the water trough. "I'm not accustomed . . ."

Shannon turned on his heel, went into the marshal's office, and slammed the door behind him.

The signs said *Firearms are prohibited in Yellow Flats. All guns must be checked at the marshal's office.* Shannon nailed one of the placards to the signpost at the eastern town limits, then rode across to do the same on the western side. Beneath each of them he fastened another one that read *Curfew 11 P.M.* Then he walked the buckskin back to the center of town and began nailing both signs beside the doors of the saloons and the town's other businesses.

As he was attaching a pair to the gatepost of the corral outside the freight office, Porter came out to see what the hammering was about. When he read the signs, he laughed.

"You don't fool around, do you?" he said to Shannon.

"You're not paying me to fool around," Shannon replied.

Porter studied his face for a few seconds.

"Are you all right?" he asked. "You look angry."

"I am angry," Shannon said.

"Why?"

"Because of what's going to happen."

"What's that?"

"You'll see."

There were seven of them when they rode in. The horseman in the lead was a heavy, scar-faced man, and as Shannon stepped off the walk into the street in front of them, he recognized from Porter's description that this was Hack Trench, the leader of the gang who had been terrorizing the town.

Trench reined up a few yards from the spot where Shannon was calmly waiting.

"Looky here, boys," Trench said over his shoulder. "Another one. This town don't learn very quick, does it?"

He turned to Shannon.

"What's this malarkey about no guns in town?" he demanded.

"New town ordinance. Marshal's office is right over there—as I think you know. Just hang your gunbelts on the rack outside the door."

"And if we don't?"

"You'll go to jail," Shannon said. "Or worse."

Trench laughed.

"You got guts, I'll say that for you. But you ain't got a brain in your head. You really think you're gonna take my gun?"

"I don't have to take it," Shannon said. "You're going to hang your gunbelt on that rack just as I said, and so are your men. Then you're welcome to enjoy the hospitality of the town until eleven P.M. After that, you can pick up your guns and ride out. That way everybody's happy, and nobody gets hurt. Is that clear, or should I go over it again for you?"

Trench's eyes narrowed.

"What's your name, lawman?" Trench asked.

"Shannon. Why?"

Trench nodded slowly.

"I heard of you," he said. "What're you doin' in a dump like this?"

"Waiting for you to check your guns," Shannon said.

"Hey, Hack," one of Trench's men said. "I know this guy. He ran me out of Ellsworth a couple of years ago. I been wantin' to meet you again, Shannon."

He rode forward and leaned his elbows on his saddlehorn.

"You figure you can outdraw all seven of us, law dog?" he said.

"What's the matter, friend?" Shannon asked with a sarcastic smile. "Don't you think you can take me by yourself?"

"Hold it, Kirk," Trench said. "I heard of this one. He ain't like the others. He's got a big rep, and he's trying to get you to draw on him."

"He is, eh?" Kirk said, straightening in the saddle. "Well, he just got his wish."

He went for his gun, but before the barrel had cleared the holster Shannon had drawn and fired. The gunman went backward over the horse's haunches and flopped down into the street, a surprised expression frozen on his face.

The outlaws' horses, frightened by the gunshot, were rearing and shying away. Their riders were momentarily occupied trying to keep the animals under control. When their horses had calmed, several of the men started to reach for their revolvers. Shannon waited patiently, his Colt cocked and ready.

"Hold it, boys," Trench said. "Keep 'em cased. I don't want to lose anybody else."

He peered down at his dead gang member and then regarded Shannon with a cold eye.

"I see how you got your reputation, Shannon," he said. "Well, you killed him, so you can bury him."

"Just him?" Shannon asked acidly.

Trench's smile was icy.

"Yeah, you win for now," he said. "We'll ride on. But we'll be back, and the next time you won't have it quite so easy."

He wheeled his horse and led his men out of town.

Attracted by the gunfire, a number of people were now coming out onto the sidewalks and into the street, staring at the dead gunman and chattering among themselves. George Porter came hurrying up the street from the freight office, and he looked relieved when he saw Shannon.

"Glad you're all right," he said. "Are they gone?"

"For now."

"You think they'll come back?"

"Oh, yes, they'll come back," Shannon said morosely. "You can bet on it. This was only round one."

He glanced at the holster just visible under Porter's coat.

"Don't forget to check your gun, Mr. Porter," he said.

Porter's mouth dropped open.

"What? Check my gun?"

Shannon pointed to one of the signs tacked to a nearby post.

"No guns in Yellow Flats," he said. "The only ones authorized to carry firearms within the town limits are myself and Deputy Ferrum—wherever he may be."

"But I hired you!" Porter said.

"I know, Mr. Porter, but the point is this—the new ordinance has to apply to everyone. If these other people see that you're obeying it, they'll respect it too because they'll realize that I'll enforce it equally against everyone. You can help me by backing me up on this."

Porter frowned in irritation, but he unbuckled his gunbelt and handed it over. Shannon turned to the watching crowd.

"Take off your guns, or get off the streets," he said. "No exceptions."

There was a low rumble of discontent from the watchers, but they moved away, some of them taking off their gunbelts as they went.

"And don't forget," Shannon called after them. "Curfew's at eleven P.M. For everybody."

Porter shook his head in amazement.

"I hope you know what you're doing," he said.

"So do I," Shannon replied.

Chapter Eighteen
Round Two

At five minutes to eleven that evening, Shannon left the office and went to both saloons to make certain that they closed down on time. Then he walked slowly through the town, looking for curfew violators. Several citizens were still abroad, and he sent them home with a sharp reminder about the new restriction. He also found two drunks passed out in the street, and these he took to jail.

When he came back into the office from the cells, Ferrum was there, waiting.

"Heard you wanted to see me," he said in a surly tone.

"That's one way of putting it," Shannon said. "We need to have a little chat."

"Yeah? What about?"

197

"You," Shannon said. "Where were you today when the Trench crowd rode in?"

"I dunno," said Ferrum. "Patrolling the other end of town, I guess."

"I don't think you've patrolled anything since you got that badge," Shannon said. "Why the town hasn't fired you long since I can't imagine. You've had a free ride up to now, but it's time for you to fish or cut bait. If you want to keep the badge, then from now on you're going to have to earn it."

"Whaddaya mean by that?"

"I mean you're going to have to start doing your job or find another one."

"So what am I supposed to do?"

"For starters, I want you here in this office every morning at eight o'clock sharp. I'll tell you then what our schedule will be for the day. And the next time there's trouble, I expect you to be there, doing whatever is necessary to stop it or back me up while I stop it. Is that clear?"

"You're the boss," Ferrum mumbled.

"That's right," Shannon said, "I am, and you either accept that or put that star on my desk right now."

"Okay, okay," Ferrum said. "I got the message."

"Fine. Then you can start work tonight. I want you to go out and check the streets for curfew violators. If you find any, send them home or bring them to me here."

Ferrum left, pouting. In half an hour he came back into the office and sank into a chair.

"This curfew idea is stupid," Ferrum said. "I sent a couple people home like you said, but they was pretty mad about it. You ain't makin' any friends this way."

"That grieves me deeply," Shannon said.

"You want me for anything else right now?" Ferrum asked.

"Yes," Shannon replied, "I want you to collect your gear from wherever it is that you spend your time and move into the office here for tonight. You can sleep on the bunk in one of the empty cells."

"But there's a couple of drunks back there. I don't wanna have to listen to them snore all night."

"Life is full of little hardships," Shannon said. "Now we'd both better get some sleep. If Trench and his pals come back tomorrow, we're going to be busy."

But Trench did not return the next day, nor the next. On the morning of the third day, Shannon was sitting at his desk when George Porter and his three associates came in.

"Look here, Shannon," Porter said, "we've gone along with your no-guns thing and this silly curfew, but people are getting tired to being cooped up in their homes at night. There hasn't been any trouble. How much longer are you going to keep it up?"

"As long as it takes."

"But what's the point?" Porter asked. "People think you're just throwing your weight around for no reason."

"Mr. Porter," Shannon said, "I know that these new

rules aren't popular. But people who don't carry guns don't start gunfights, and the curfew will keep the streets clear late in the evening. Both of those things will drastically cut down on the amount of trouble we're likely to have around here. Furthermore, when Trench and his hoodlums come back there'll probably be gunplay, and then the people who are grumbling now will be very glad they're safe at home, out of the line of fire."

Porter nodded slowly.

"Okay," he said. "I see your point. Come on, gentlemen, let's go back to our businesses and let the marshal get on with his job."

Shannon made his usual eleven o'clock patrol of the town but found it quiet.

This is what they wanted, he reminded himself, *and now they all hate me for it.*

He returned to his office, checked to be sure that the windows were securely shut and the door locked behind him, and sat down at his desk. He had not been sleeping well—recurrent nightmares made his rest uneasy and fragmented—and before long he began to doze, sitting in his chair.

At 12:23 A.M. gunfire erupted in the street outside the office, and bullets exploded through the shutters and door. One slug broke a shutter latch, and the shutter flew open, exposing Shannon to full view from the street. Splinters of glass and wood flew across the room as Shannon hit the floor and rolled behind the desk. One of the oil lamps hanging on the wall opposite the door disintegrated, spraying kerosene over the wall and floor.

Just don't let it burn, Shannon thought. *It's going to be hot enough in here as it is.*

He reached up and snatched a shotgun from the rack beside his desk. Bullets were still buzzing through the office, many of them hitting the opposite wall and the door to the jail.

"Ferrum!" Shannon shouted. "Are you all right?"

The deputy had been asleep in one of the cells, but there was no reply to his hail. *Maybe he's hit,* Shannon thought. Then he heard the sound of footsteps running away through the jail. Shannon could hear the back door of the jail opening, and someone hurrying through it. Then the footsteps faded as the back door slammed shut again. Ferrum had fled into the night.

Muzzle flashes continued to light up the street, and lead was still flying through the office. Several bullets had already hit the desk behind which Shannon was sheltering, and he knew that it was only a matter of time before one found him. He reached up from the floor to open his desk drawer, and extracted a handful of shotgun shells. He shoved them into his pocket and leaped up from behind the desk, firing through the open shutter into the street. A scream told him that at least some of the buckshot had found its mark.

He ran across the room toward the door, ramming

new shells into the shotgun. As he came outside, he could make out five riders in the street, all firing their six-guns at the office. A sixth horse was bolting away, its rider knocked out of the saddle by Shannon's first shot. Shannon fired again, and two more riders went down, shrieking. A bullet went through the fabric of Shannon's shirt and burned along his side. He ignored the pain and, drawing his six-gun, shot a fourth man out of his saddle. The two remaining gunmen jerked their horses' heads around and fled at a gallop into the night. Shannon threw two quick shots after them, but they were already lost in the darkness.

Shannon waited on the walk outside the office for a moment, letting his pulse rate and breathing subside. He noted with some amusement that despite the fusillade of gunfire, no one came out into the street to see what had happened.

At least they're obeying the curfew, he thought. *Maybe they appreciate its value a little more now.*

At that moment footsteps echoed down the boardwalk, and George Porter appeared out of the dark. He was carrying a shotgun and was out of breath from running.

"You can arrest me for breaking the curfew if you want to," he puffed, "but I had to see if you were all right."

"Under the circumstances," Shannon said, "I'll overlook the violation."

They examined the men lying in the street. All were dead.

"You're certainly efficient with your ammunition," Porter said. "Four for four, looks like."

"Buckshot sometimes makes up for bad aim," Shannon said. "It's a good thing Trench only sent a few men, though. Next time, he'll bring the whole gang."

Porter went off to find the town's carpenter, who doubled as undertaker of Yellow Flats.

Shannon went back into the office and checked the jail. Except for the two drunks, the cells were empty. Deputy Marshal Ferrum had indeed run out the back door when the shooting started.

Six-gun ready, Shannon went out the back door into the alley and looked around. Someone was crouched down behind a group of trash cans a few feet from the back door of the jail, and in the light coming through from inside, Shannon could see that it was Ferrum. He holstered his revolver and walked over to the spot where Ferrum was hiding. He kicked the trash cans out of the way and grabbed Ferrum by the shirt front, lifting the cowering deputy to his feet. Shannon drew back his fist and drove it into Ferrum's stomach, knocking him sprawling on the ground. As Shannon advanced on him again, Ferrum began to whimper with fear, begging Shannon not to hit him again.

Wordlessly, Shannon reached down and tore the deputy's star off Ferrum's shirt. Ferrum squealed in terror and began to grovel at Shannon's feet. Shannon contemplated this spectacle in silence for a few seconds, then turned and walked back to the jail. In the doorway, he paused and looked back to where Ferrum still lay squirming in the dirt.

"By the way," he said to Ferrum, "you're fired."

Morning found the bodies gone from the street in front of the office—the carpenter had removed them during the night. From the carpenter shop the sound of sawing and hammering could be heard.

Porter came into Shannon's office.

"Coffins," he said, jerking his thumb toward the noise.

Shannon tossed him the badge he had torn off Ferrum's shirt.

"Deputy Marshal Ferrum has handed in his resignation," he said.

Porter laughed.

"I saw him going into the saloon this morning," he said, "and I wondered why his shirt pocket was torn. Now I know. You want another deputy? You can swear me in, if you like. I'm no lawman, but I'll do what I can to help."

"No," said Shannon, shaking his head. "I appreciate the offer, but I don't want you taking that risk. I'll handle this by myself."

"I'd better tell you," Porter said, "that a lot of people are upset about the shooting last night. They're afraid that Trench and his men will come gunning for you again, and take it out on the town."

"They wanted Trench's gang run out or wiped out," Shannon said. "Last night was part of the process."

"I'm not arguing with you," said Porter hastily. "I'm just telling you what people are saying."

"Of course," Shannon said. "It's exactly what I expected them to say."

"What now?"

"Breakfast," Shannon said wearily.

Several cups of coffee and a generous helping of bacon and eggs revived Shannon somewhat, but he could feel the fatigue building up in him, and it was evident from the demeanor of the café staff and the other customers that Porter was right about the feelings of the locals. The waitress barely spoke to him, and the people sitting at the other tables glanced at him out of the corners of their eyes with obvious antagonism.

He paid for his meal and started back for the marshal's office. As he approached the office door, someone stepped out into the street in front of him. It was Ferrum.

"Hold it, Shannon," Ferrum shouted when Shannon was about fifty feet from him. "You and me gotta settle this right now."

"There's nothing to settle," Shannon said calmly. "You're fired. Period."

"Nobody treats me like that," Ferrum snarled. "I'm gonna kill you, Shannon. I'm gonna show this whole town that I'm a better man than you. Then you'll be dead and I'll be the marshal of Yellow Flats."

"You're drunk, Ferrum," Shannon said. "Go back to the saloon before you get hurt."

"Not a chance," Ferrum said. He looked around at the people who were now gathering on the boardwalk to gawk at the two men in the street. "Watch this, you sniveling jackasses," he bellowed. "I'll show you who should be the marshal here."

He faced Shannon with his hand hovering over his holster.

"Come on, Shannon," he said. "Draw!"

Shannon took a deep breath.

"Don't be a fool, man," he said. "I don't want to have to kill you. Walk away, and be glad you're alive and out of this in one piece."

"Draw!" Ferrum screamed.

"Back off, Ferrum," Shannon said desperately. "You haven't got a chance."

"If you won't draw, I will!" Ferrum cried. His hand went to his gun, and he brought the weapon out of the holster, pointing it at Shannon.

"Draw, or I'll shoot you down where you stand," Ferrum said, cocking the hammer. His hand was shaking so badly he could hardly hold the heavy revolver.

"Put it down, Ferrum," Shannon said. "Don't do this."

Ferrum fired. The bullet missed Shannon's head by a fraction of an inch. Ferrum cocked the hammer again, and raised the six-gun to take dead aim at Shannon's face.

"I won't miss this time," Ferrum bawled. "You're dead, Shannon."

As Ferrum spoke, Shannon drew and fired. Ferrum pulled the trigger of his weapon, but the shot went wild, and he staggered backward as Shannon's bullet hit him high on the right side of his chest. The ex-deputy fell to his knees, then keeled over into the dirt. He lay there on his side, trying again to cock the hammer of his six-gun. Shannon leaped forward and kicked the gun out of his hand.

"You . . ." Ferrum said, and fell back, unconscious.

People were gathering around, trying to see what had happened.

"Somebody help me get him out of the street," Shannon said, holstering the Colt. Nobody moved. Shannon picked Ferrum up on his own and took him into the marshal's office, stretching him out on the bunk.

George Porter came in.

"How is he?" Porter asked.

"Alive," Shannon said. "But just barely."

"I'll get a couple of my men and we'll take him over to his room," Porter said. "I've already sent someone to find the doctor."

"I don't think it's going to do much good," Shannon said. He found that he was shaking, and a sudden, terrible image flashed through his mind as he saw once more the young Randy Cutler lying mortally wounded on the floor of the saloon back in Cauldron County just a few short months ago. *At least that was an accident,* Shannon thought. *I shot this one on purpose. And for what?*

Porter's men took Ferrum away, and Shannon sat at his desk, his head in his hands, waiting. An hour later, Porter came back into the office.

"He's dead," he said simply.

"I'm sorry to hear it," Shannon said. "I didn't want to kill him."

"The way you let him keep shooting at you before you finally drew," said Porter, "you're lucky to be alive."

"Yes," Shannon said. "Lucky."

The town was soon abuzz with the news of the killing of Jake Ferrum. The stares that followed Shannon as he made his rounds that afternoon were now openly resentful. Shannon understood their antagonism. The other men he had shot had been part of the Trench gang—the town's tormentors and enemies. Ferrum, whatever else he was, had been a resident of Yellow Flats, and Shannon—the stranger among them—had killed him.

Porter was waiting for Shannon in the marshal's office.

"I'd watch my back for a while, if I were you," Porter said. "A couple of the locals are grumbling about your shooting Ferrum. Right now if we had a popularity contest between you and Hack Trench, Trench might win."

"No doubt," Shannon said. "Anybody in particular showing signs of wanting to avenge Model Citizen Ferrum's demise?"

"I don't know," Porter said. "Maybe. Every town has its loudmouths and its would-be gunslingers, and Yellow Flats is no exception. They all crawl into the woodwork when the Trench gang is around, but there are certainly a couple who would be happy to backshoot you. Some drunks down at the Green Lantern have been sounding off about you killing Ferrum, and the Rathole has a few regular customers who might just give you trouble if they don't pass out under the table first."

He paused.

"I guess the one that I'd really keep an eye out for is Ferrum's nephew, a kid named Joe Treadle. He's Ferrum's sister's boy. Typical teenage hooligan. He's barely started to shave, but he thinks he's tough, and packs twin revolvers looking for a chance to prove it."

Shannon nodded. "I know the type," he said. "Thanks for the warning."

He leaned forward on the desk and rested his head on his arms.

Just what I need, he said to himself. *First Ferrum, now a gun-happy juvenile delinquent with a grudge. And I thought the Trench gang was going to be my only problem.* Somehow he knew that sooner or later he would meet Joe Treadle, and he was already dreading it.

The meeting was not long in coming. Shannon had walked out of the office to start his evening tour of the town, and was just crossing the street when a shrill adolescent voice stopped him.

"Turn around, big man," the speaker said. "I'm gonna cut you down to size."

Shannon knew before he turned that he was about to make Joe Treadle's acquaintance.

Ferrum's nephew was as Shannon had pictured him—thin, rat-faced like his uncle, sporting a wispy mustache that was intended to make him look older but in fact made him look ridiculous. He was packing two guns tied so low on his hips that it was a wonder that he could even reach them—a frequent mistake of would-be gunfighters. Treadle was standing in the street a few yards away from Shannon, both arms bent so that his hands hovered dramatically above his holsters.

"Go home, son," Shannon said. "You don't need this kind of trouble."

"Don't tell me what I need," said Treadle. "You killed my Uncle Jake, and I'm gonna kill you."

"I'm sorry about that, son," Shannon said patiently. "I didn't want to hurt him. He forced it on me, and I had no choice."

"You could have shot the gun out of his hand instead of killing him," Treadle snarled.

"That's dime novel stuff, son," Shannon said. "If you live long enough to be the badman you think you already are, you'll learn that in a gunfight there's no time for fancy tricks like aiming at somebody's gun hand. When a man draws on you, you have only one choice—to stop him from killing you. And the only way to do that with any certainty is to hit him in the body. That may seem harsh, but it's true. Anybody who tries to shoot a gun out of somebody's hand is going to wind up dead, sooner rather than later. So, as I said, I had no choice. Your uncle forced the play, and I did what I had to do. Again, I'm sorry it happened."

"Well, now I'm gonna do what I have to do," Treadle said, his hands inching down toward his guns. "Go for your gun!"

"Listen to me, Treadle," Shannon said in exasperation, "there's a kid like you in every town in the West, somebody who thinks he's going to make a big reputation by outdrawing a well-known lawman or gunfighter. Mostly, punks like that end up dead in some dirty gutter because they thought that drawing a gun in front of a bedroom mirror was the same as facing an armed man in the street."

"I ain't gonna wind up like that," Treadle said truculently. "Not today, anyway."

"Maybe not," Shannon agreed. "Sometimes kids like you get lucky, get away with it the first time at least, get that big reputation they want so much. But then they're marked men, people who'll never know a moment's peace again, because after that they'll be the targets of every gun-packing troublemaker who wants to make his own reputation at their expense. Eventually, as sure as night follows day, they'll meet up with someone faster than they are. Remember that, Joe. No matter how fast you are, *there's always someone faster.*"

"You ain't so fast, Shannon," Treadle said with contempt. "You was slow as molasses when you shot Uncle Jake."

"There's a difference between slow and reluctant," Shannon said. "I didn't want to kill your uncle, and I gave him the chance to back off before it was too late. Don't count on that happening again."

"Aw shut up," Treadle squeaked. "All you do is talk. Now reach for that fancy six-gun of yours or I'll plug you anyway."

Shannon sighed. This was like some bad dream that he had lived through again and again—and now he was living through it twice in one day, with someone whom he did not want to harm trying to goad him into gunplay. He had already killed one member of this family, and he did not want to kill another.

He started walking toward Treadle, keeping his hand well clear of his holster. Treadle's eyes grew wide.

"Stop right there!" he cried. "I'll draw on you if you take another step!"

"Go ahead," Shannon said, still moving forward. "What's stopping you?"

He was within a few feet of Treadle now, his eyes locked with the youngster's, for he knew that Treadle's eyes would tell him what he needed to know. At first Treadle hesitated, and Shannon thought that perhaps Treadle would back down. Then, when he was only a step away, he saw Treadle's expression harden as the boy made up his mind.

Too late, Joe, Shannon thought. *You waited too long.*

Treadle's hands dipped down toward his guns. Shannon grabbed him by the shoulders and whirled him around, then kicked him hard in the backside, knocking him over on his face in the street. One of Treadle's revolvers went spinning away to land in the dirt, but even as he fell he was still trying to draw the other. Shannon brought his heel down hard on Treadle's gun arm, pinning it to the ground, then reached over and pulled the six-gun from the youngster's fingers.

The boy lay there gasping for breath, the wind knocked out of him by Shannon's well-placed blow and his collision with the ground.

"No fair!" he whined, rolling over and glaring at Shannon. "You kicked me!"

"My apologies," Shannon said. "Next time I'll shoot you instead."

He pulled Treadle to his feet.

"Go home, sonny," he said, "and thank your lucky stars you're still alive."

"What about my guns?"

"I'll keep them in the marshal's office until you grow up. You can come and get them then."

He spun Treadle around and shoved him away. Treadle limped off down the street, rubbing his sore backside. After a few steps, he turned around and shook his fist at Shannon.

"This ain't over," he cried. "You made a fool outta me, and I won't forget it."

"You're wrong, Joe," Shannon said gently, "I didn't

make a fool out of you. You made a fool out of yourself. Try to keep that in mind."

When Treadle was out of sight, Shannon picked up the two revolvers and started back for the marshal's office. One of the people who had watched the episode from the safety of the sidewalk called to him as he passed.

"You think you're tough, don't you Shannon?" the man said. "First you push us around, now you start beating up our kids."

"Tell your kids not to play with guns," Shannon replied. "They'll live longer."

Chapter Nineteen
Retribution

"Come in, gentlemen," Shannon said, looking up from his desk. "I've been expecting you."

The five men crowded into the little office, looking nervous but determined. Shannon recognized the two saloon owners, the owner of the mercantile store, and two other merchants. George Porter came in the door behind them and leaned against the wall, looking unhappy.

The owner of the Green Lantern Saloon spoke first.

"Mr. Shannon," he said, "we think things have gone far enough. This curfew is hurting our business, and we want all this killing to stop."

"You and your associates told me that you wanted Trench's gang run out of town or killed," Shannon said. "So far I've fulfilled your wishes to the tune of five dead men. I'd say you're getting you're money's worth."

"Oh, certainly," said the saloon owner quickly. "We agree, absolutely. And we appreciate what you've done. That's why I've been empowered by the business owners of Yellow Flats to pay you the remainder of your fee now and discharge you from any further responsibility to the town."

He placed four hundred dollars on the desk, pulling his hand back quickly as if afraid that Shannon might bite him.

Shannon looked at Porter.

"You in on this, Mr. Porter?" he asked.

"No," Porter said sourly. "I got outvoted."

"I see," Shannon said. "So this is the result of a vote, is it?"

He stood up, took the money from the desktop, and tucked it firmly into the saloon owner's coat pocket.

"You forget, gentlemen," he said, "that there's only one vote that counts here, and that's mine. When you offered me this job, you agreed to several conditions, one of which was that you wouldn't interfere with me until the job was done. Well, the job isn't done yet. The Trench gang isn't going to just vanish into the desert now. In fact, after last night they're going to come at me again, and they'll come in full force this time."

"That's just the point," said the mercantile store owner in his squeaky voice. "We're afraid of what they'll do to the town."

"That's precisely why I can't quit," Shannon said. "I took an oath to defend Yellow Flats, and I mean to keep that oath. When they come again, I'll be here to stop them."

"But we don't *want* you here anymore," said the owner of the Rathole Saloon.

"I know," Shannon said, "but we town tamers have a certain code of ethics that I have to uphold. Our agreement was that I wouldn't quit until this was over, and I'm bound by that agreement. So you see, as much as I'd like to leave, I have no choice but to stay and see things through. Good day, gentlemen."

Shannon finished repairing the office's broken shutter and the damaged front door just before sundown. After putting away the tools, he went down the street to the café to eat a solitary meal. It was dark when he came out, and he walked slowly back toward the office, pondering the events of the day.

Trench would come again, he knew. The question was when, and how. *And with how many,* he added to himself. Somehow, he would have to gain an advantage over what was bound to be superior numbers. But how could he do that?

He felt, rather than heard, the movement on the boardwalk behind him. Someone had come out of the shadows of an alley he had just passed, someone that Shannon could see only in silhouette in the darkness. He wheeled around to defend himself, but even as his hand touched the Colt ivory grips, he knew he was going to be too late.

The boom of the shotgun reverberated off the wooden

walls of the street, and the muzzle flash lit up the scene in an unreal glare. Shannon felt the shot tearing into his left thigh and knee. He fell face-down on the boardwalk, feeling the searing pain of the wound and the warmth of his own blood soaking his leg. The silhouette was still there, raising the shotgun to fire again. Shannon had just time to pull the trigger of the Colt once before he found himself plummeting sickeningly down into the vast black void of unconsciousness.

"I think he's coming out of it," the voice said. "Marshal, can you hear me?"

Shannon opened his eyes and found himself lying in a bed in a room dimly lit by a single oil lamp. In its glow, he could see two figures bending over him.

"Where . . . ?" he mumbled.

"It's all right," said the voice. "You're in my spare bedroom. Doc Wilson's here too."

Shannon realized that the speaker was George Porter, and recognized the other man as the town doctor.

"My leg," he said, craning his neck to look down along the sheets toward his left knee.

"It's broken," Doctor Wilson said. "You took some buckshot in it, but they missed the artery. You're going to be laid up for a while, but you should be able to walk again in a few weeks."

"Anybody see who did it?"

"No," Porter replied. "He got away. You winged him, though, with that one shot you got off. He turned and ran after you fired at him. We found a blood trail leading back into the alley. Nice shooting, under the circumstances."

Shannon lay back on the pillow. His leg was starting to hurt badly.

"Guess I should have quit this job when I had the chance," he said, forcing a thin laugh.

"Well, you're temporarily retired now," the doctor said. "I've given you some laudanum, and I'm going to leave a bottle here on the bedside table. It'll help when the pain gets rough. Porter, is somebody going to be here to look after him for a few days?"

"The old woman who keeps house for me since my wife died will take care of him, and I'll look in every chance I get," Porter replied.

"Then I'd better get going," Wilson said, snapping shut his medical bag. "Got a baby on the way on the other side of town, and it's not going to wait on me indefinitely. Marshal, I'll check in on you later tonight or tomorrow morning, whenever I get back."

"Thanks, Doc," Shannon said. "Sorry to be a nuisance."

"You haven't been much trouble up to now," the doctor said. "Usually the only person you create any work for is the carpenter."

"The carpenter?" Shannon said, still trying to focus his thoughts.

"He makes the town's coffins," said Porter, "remember?"

Chapter Twenty
Alone

Shannon remembered little about the next few days. It was a time of pain and fever and nightmarish dreams, dreams of gun flashes and dead faces and sinister shadows hovering around him in the darkness. Then, gradually, as the days crawled slowly by, the fever subsided and the nightmares diminished, and more and more often he found himself able to eat the meals that George Porter's housekeeper brought in to him.

Porter himself was a frequent visitor to the bedroom, as was the town doctor.

"How does it look, Doc?" Shannon asked during one of these visits, as the doctor finished changing the bandage on his knee.

"It's healing," the doctor said. "You aren't going to be going dancing for a while yet, though."

"How much longer before I can get out of this bed?"

"Couple of weeks, I'd say. Don't rush it, Mr. Shannon. If you try to put weight on that leg too soon, you could make yourself lame for the rest of your life."

"Did anybody ever find out who ambushed me?"

"Afraid not," Porter said. "Curious thing, though— we know you at least creased whoever did it when you fired at him, and Joe Treadle was walking around for a couple of days after that with a sore arm."

"Treadle?" said the doctor. "He wouldn't have the guts to do something like this."

"Doesn't take much guts to bushwhack a man," Porter said. "But the truth is, it might have been anybody. Shannon's not exactly the town's best-loved resident. Could have been one of Trench's thugs too. Backshooting would be about their style."

"It warms my heart that I have so many friends in this community," Shannon said caustically. "It also sounds as if I'll never be able to prove who ambushed me. It could have been Treadle—he certainly has a grudge against me for his uncle and for the way I humiliated the kid in public. But the odds are it was Trench's people who did this, and if it was, they'll try again, so I may have a chance to square things with them."

"Not for a while yet, you won't," the doctor said. "I don't want you going on any manhunts until that leg mends."

"Doc's right," Porter said. "You'd better take it easy for a bit longer."

He placed several books on the bedside table.

"Here," he said, "I brought you some things to read. "Shakespeare, some English poetry, and a couple of dime novels for excitement. You're in one of them, by the way."

"I am?" Shannon said, puzzled.

"Yeah, a story by some writer named Peabody, who claims to have interviewed you back in Kansas. All about how you single-handedly cleaned up the West. Didn't know we had a celebrity on our hands here."

"Blast that idiot," Shannon said. "I told him to write about Cash Bonham."

"Oh, Bonham's in there too," Porter chuckled. "Something about you and him fighting off a hundred bandits in a schoolhouse in Longhorn."

Shannon shook his head in disgust.

"There were only four of them," he said, "and they were drunk."

"Enjoy your fame," Porter said. "They tell me it doesn't last long."

"*Sic transit gloria mundi,*" quoted the doctor, "which, loosely translated, means *'All glory is fleeting.'* "

"You've got that right," Shannon said with feeling.

The night was hot, a breathless late-summer evening when no breeze stirred the curtains of the open window of Shannon's bedroom. Shannon lay on the bed, the discomfort of the dull ache in his leg accentuated by the rivulets of sweat trickling down his back, soaking the sheets beneath him.

I've got to get out of this bed soon, he thought, *or I'll go crazy. Come on, leg, heal.*

His thoughts were interrupted by a small but perceptible motion of the curtains. There was no breeze to cause the movement, and even Shannon's mind, dulled from pain, was suddenly alert.

Someone's out there, he thought. The bedroom in which he lay was on the ground floor, which placed the window within easy reach of any potential intruder. Shannon had put out the lamp earlier in the evening in a futile effort to mitigate the heat of the room, so he now lay in darkness, his eyes already accustomed to the gloom.

The curtain moved again. Shannon reached under his pillow and brought out the Colt revolver. Slowly and quietly he drew back the hammer until the tiny click told him that it was in the full cocked position. Then he waited, hardly daring to breathe.

A hand appeared, pulling back the curtain, and Shannon could just discern a shadowy form standing outside the window. Then the long silhouette of a shotgun barrel came snaking through the curtains, slowly rotating toward the spot where Shannon lay.

Shannon fired. Someone screamed and the shotgun fell heavily onto the windowsill, discharging its load of buckshot into the bedroom ceiling. Immediately a

man came leaping through the window, firing random-
ly around the room. Shannon put two slugs into the
shadowy figure, causing it to drop to the floor.
Someone still outside the window fired through it; the
bullet narrowly missed Shannon's face and plowed
into the head of the bed beside his pillow. Shannon
rolled out of the bed onto the floor, biting back a cry
of pain as his injured leg struck the floorboards.
Another bullet sang past him, and he raised the six-
gun and fired twice more through the open window.
He was rewarded with a howl of pain from someone
outside, and then a string of curses was followed by
the sound of creaking saddle leather. Immediately
thereafter, hoofbeats could be heard fading away into
the night.

Shannon remained on the floor for a few seconds,
catching his breath and waiting for the pain in his leg to
subside. Then he grasped the edge of the bedstead and
pulled himself back onto the bed. Gritting his teeth, he
pushed himself up off the bed and staggered three steps
to the window. Outside there was no one to be seen.
Whoever had attacked him had survived and escaped.

The door of the bedroom burst open and Porter came
in, holding a lamp in one hand and a six-gun in the
other.

"Easy," Shannon said. "They've gone—what's left
of them."

By the light of Porter's lamp, they examined the
body on the floor.

"Recognize him?" Porter asked.

"Yes," Shannon said. "It's one of Trench's men. I think I got one more—he may be on the ground outside."

Porter peered cautiously through the window.

"Yeah, you got him. He's lying right underneath the window. Looks like he's dead too."

Shannon lay back on the bed, overcome by the weakness of his body.

"I heard horses," he said, "at least two."

"Seems like Trench is really carrying a grudge against you," Porter mused. "He's waited nearly three weeks and then tried to kill you while you were lying helpless in bed. Well," he added, looking at the dead man on the bedroom floor, "not quite helpless, I guess. Too bad some of them got away."

"Don't worry," Shannon said. "They'll be back."

Shannon was awakened the next morning by the sounds of heated conversation in the hall outside his bedroom.

"But he's got to *do* something," a shrill voice insisted.

"The man's wounded," Porter's voice said. "He can't even walk yet. What do you expect him to do?"

"We don't care what he does," another voice replied, "but he's got to help us. Trench and his gang are bound to come back now for sure."

"George," Shannon called, "bring the gentlemen in."

They filed into the bedroom, a delegation of three led by the owner of the Green Lantern Saloon.

Shannon sat up in the bed, regarding them with a mixture of amusement and contempt.

"So, what seems to be the problem today?" he asked.

"You know what the problem is," the saloon keeper huffed. "Now that you've killed two more of Trench's men, he's surely going to come back with his whole gang looking for revenge. Why did you have to shoot those people last night?"

"It seemed logical at the time," Shannon said.

"Yes, but what do we do now? We paid you to protect us, not cause more trouble. Trench's probably got another eight or ten men left in his gang, and he's likely to bring them all this time."

"It certainly presents a challenge," Shannon said with irony. "Let me think about it for a bit. Thank you for your visit, gentlemen."

When they had gone, Porter came back into the room.

"I apologize for those idiots," he said. "They make me sick. They've got a point, though—you can't fight off the entire gang from that bed. Maybe we'd better put you in one of my freight wagons and get you out of town."

"No," Shannon said. "That would just put your freighters in danger too. But there is a way you can help. Could you send a couple of men out to each end of town to watch the road coming in? I don't want them to fight—just act as lookouts. I need to have some warning when Trench is on his way in again."

"Consider it done. When they spot the gang, what do you want them to do?"

"Just come and warn me."

"That's all?"

"Yes. That's all."

He lay back on the bed and closed his eyes, contemplating his own mortality.

They came shortly after noon the next day. Porter's lookout ran breathlessly into the bedroom to announce that he had seen nine men riding over the salt flats toward town.

"How far away are they?" Shannon asked.

"About a mile. They ain't in any hurry, I guess—they was just walking their horses along the road, bold as you please, like they was on their way to a picnic."

"All right," Shannon said, "thanks. Now get out of sight and stay there. The rest is up to me."

Shannon had risen from the bed at dawn and dressed himself. After strapping on his gunbelt he had lain back down, waiting for the news he was sure would come. Now he rose again, pulling himself painfully erect and reaching for the crutch that the doctor had provided in anticipation of the day that Shannon would walk again.

Porter watched the process with undisguised skepticism.

"Clay, you can't do this," Porter said. "You can't walk, much less dodge or run. How are you going to deal with nine gunmen?"

"I won't be dodging or running," Shannon said, "so that part won't make any difference. But there isn't much time. Help me get to my office."

With the assistance of Porter and the crutch, Shannon limped painfully down the street to the marshal's office. Climbing the steps was difficult, and by the time he reached the chair behind his desk, he was perspiring profusely from effort and pain.

"Thanks," Shannon said, as Porter helped him ease down into the chair. "Now go back to the freight office and stay there. Don't try to help when the shooting starts—I mean it. I'll be all right."

Porter started to protest, but Shannon cut him off.

"Go on, George. I don't have time to argue with you."

Porter departed, shaking his head

As soon as Porter was out of the office, Shannon stood up and removed his rifle from the wall rack. Tucking a box of ammunition in his pocket, he grabbed the crutch and started for the door. He crossed the street in slow, painful steps, pausing twice to brace himself for the next attempt. As he entered the hotel, the desk clerk looked up at him in surprise.

"Have you eaten lunch yet?" Shannon asked.

The puzzled clerk replied that he had not.

"Then go now," Shannon said, "and don't come back for at least an hour. There's going to be some shooting, and you don't want to be in here when it starts. Understand?"

The desk clerk gulped, nodded vigorously, and departed out the hotel's back door. Shannon attempted to ascend the stairs to the hotel's second floor, but found that he could not manage the rifle, the crutch, and the steps all at the same time. He tossed the crutch over the banister and proceeded to drag himself up, one step at a time, to the hotel's second floor. In the second floor hallway, he found the ladder that led to the roof. Putting his weight only on his good leg, and using his arms to pull himself up each succeeding rung, he inched up the ladder. At the top, he pushed open the trapdoor and crawled out onto the flat surface of the hotel's roof, nearly exhausted by the effort.

The roof was covered with sunbaked black tar paper, and the midday heat radiating off of it was like a blow in Shannon's face. He lay on the roof by the trapdoor for several seconds, gasping for breath in the super- heated air and trying to ignore the pain of his leg. He would have liked to rest there for a moment, but he knew that he was almost out of time and had to keep moving.

Ahead of him, on the west side of the roof, a small water cistern—really little more than a large rain barrel—rested on the flat roof. It was placed there to provide a reservoir of water for the bathroom on the hotel's second floor directly beneath it. This was the object of Shannon's painful journey, for during the hours of the preceding night, he had planned his cam- paign carefully. Now he had almost reached his goal, but he was not quite there yet—he had another twenty feet to cover across the scalding tarpaper, and the seconds were ticking away.

He dragged himself hand over hand along the roof to the cistern, and looked around the side of it. As he had anticipated, because the cistern was near the edge of the roof he could shelter behind it while having an unimpeded view of the west part of town and the main street below.

He had reached the cistern's protective cover none too soon, for the nine horsemen that the lookout had reported were at that moment entering the west edge of Yellow Flats. They reined up near the town limits sign with its subsidiary signs regarding firearms and the curfew. For several seconds they amused themselves by firing at the sign until it fell off the post, a splintered wreck.

Keep it up, boys, Shannon thought. *The more ammunition you waste on those signs, the less you'll have to fire at me.*

The riders now resumed their journey down the main street, and soon reached a point barely fifty yards from the hotel. Hack Trench was in the lead, with his men grouped close behind him.

First rule is, Hack old buddy, Shannon thought, *don't bunch up. Makes it easy for ruthless people like me.*

Shannon levered a shell into the chamber of the rifle and, still lying beside the water cistern, drew a careful bead on Trench's chest. Then, just for an instant, he hesitated. He had never before fired on any outlaw without first giving the man a chance to surrender. But these men had come to kill him—had already tried to kill him, in fact—and he was outnumbered nine-to-one. To give warning would be suicidal. His only chance of survival was to take his would-be assassins by surprise. He had no alternative.

Shannon pulled the trigger, and the rifle cracked, causing the noise to echo along the street. Trench had turned in his saddle just as Shannon fired, and for a moment Shannon thought he had missed. Then Trench toppled out of his saddle and fell heavily to the ground.

The remaining outlaws were thrown into a panic by the unexpected shooting of their leader. Fighting to control their frightened horses, they looked around wildly for the source of the gunshot, but there was a hot wind blowing off the desert that afternoon, and it had carried away the smoke from Shannon's rifle before the astonished outlaws could pinpoint his location. Several of them began firing wildly around the street, which further panicked their horses. As the animals reared and plunged, Shannon fired again and again. Within the space of ten seconds from the moment that he had fired the first shot, four more of Trench's men had been knocked out of their saddles by Shannon's deadly aim.

But now the gunsmoke had given away Shannon's position, and the remaining gunmen were leaping out of their saddles, returning fire with their six-guns as they ran for cover. One outlaw paused to pull his rifle out of his saddle scabbard as he dismounted and started to run. The decision to reach for the rifle delayed his escape just long enough for Shannon to bring him down two strides short of the boardwalk.

The three remaining outlaws were blazing away at Shannon, and bullets were hitting the water cistern. One shot knocked splinters off the staves, stinging Shannon's face. Several other slugs penetrated the wood of the cistern, and sun-heated water spurted out, creating a puddle that began to spread across the roof.

The outlaw Shannon had just shot near the boardwalk was now squirming along on his stomach in the dust of the street, trying to reach safety. Shannon fired at him a second time, and he did not move again.

Two of the three unwounded outlaws had sought shelter in doorways across the street from the hotel, and the roof over the boardwalk in front of the doorways hid them from Shannon's view. The third man, less prudent, had dived behind a water trough and kept popping up to throw shots at Shannon before ducking back behind the trough. Just as the outlaw's bullets could not penetrate the cistern behind which Shannon was lying, so too Shannon's bullets could only punch holes in the side of the water trough near the gunman. However, as the water ran out of the trough through the holes, the water level lowered, and when he judged that the level was low enough, Shannon fired three quick rounds through the wooden sides of the half-emptied trough. At least one of the bullets penetrated both sides of the trough, because he heard a shrill cry from behind it. The man who had been hiding there leaped up, grasping at his stomach. Shannon shot him again, and he fell backward to lie spreadeagled against the edge of the boardwalk.

But Shannon was facing the same problem—the water was rapidly draining out of the cistern behind which he had taken cover, and soon the water level would be low enough that the next shots from the street might well go all the way through the cistern to strike him. However, the two remaining gunmen either did not think of this or did not care to wait that long, because they suddenly burst out of the doorways where they had been sheltering and raced across the street toward the hotel. Before Shannon could draw a bead on either of them, they had passed out of his line of sight onto the covered boardwalk immediately in front of the hotel.

Shannon knew that if the two men caught him out on the flat roof, exposed to their fire, he would have little chance, so he pulled himself back across the sweltering roof to the trap door. Putting the rifle down on the hot, sticky tar paper, Shannon drew his six-gun and waited, watching through the trapdoor as the two gunmen came pounding up the hotel stairs and into the second-floor hall below him. One of them made the mistake of running under the trapdoor and looking up. Shannon shot him, and he crumpled to the floor at the foot of the ladder. The remaining man jumped back out of view and began firing up through the ceiling of the second floor. The roof beams stopped some of the bullets, but two came through, punching holes in the tar paper within inches of Shannon's head.

Shannon flattened out on the tar paper, being careful to make no sound. The extreme heat of the roof was causing him to perspire freely, but he made no attempt to wipe away the rivulets of sweat coursing down his face.

"Hey, Shannon!" the gunman cried. "You dead yet?"

Shannon said nothing, waiting.

The sounds from below told Shannon that the man was now slowly climbing the ladder toward the trap-door. Suddenly a pair of eyes appeared above the level of the roof. They widened for an instant as their owner saw the muzzle of Shannon's six-gun pointed at them, a matter of inches away. Shannon shot the man through the forehead, and he went crashing down the ladder to lie crumpled on the floor next to the other man.

Now nearly fainting from exhaustion and the unbearable heat, Shannon dragged himself over the edge of the trap door and managed to get down the ladder to the second floor hall. He bent over the bodies of the two men he had shot through the trapdoor, but both were dead.

Slowly moving as if in a dream, Shannon holstered the Colt and started painfully down the stairs to the hotel lobby. He found the crutch where he had left it at the bottom of the stairs and struggled across the lobby to the front door of the hotel. As he came out onto the boardwalk, he looked around him. Six bodies lay in the street where Shannon's bullets had deposited them. Shannon started to limp across to see if any of the men were still alive, but as he reached the middle of the street, he stopped suddenly. Six bodies. There should have been seven.

"I'm right here, Shannon," a gravely voice said behind him. "Turn around so I can see the look on your face when I plug you."

Shannon let the crutch fall and turned around, tottering unsteadily as he stood there, alone, in the middle of the street. Hack Trench was on the boardwalk, leaning heavily against the front wall of the hotel. His left arm was hanging loosely at his side, and his left sleeve and the left side of his shirt and pants were soaked with blood. Bloodstains smeared the wall against which he was resting.

"Did you get them all?" Trench asked. "All my people?"

Shannon nodded wordlessly.

"I underestimated you, Shannon," Trench said with disgust. "The first day I laid eyes on you, I had a dozen men in my gang. Now there's just me left. I guess I should say congratulations or something, but instead I'm going to kill you right here in the street, just like you killed my friends."

He extended his right arm, pointing his six-gun at Shannon's stomach. His thumb drew back the hammer, and Shannon saw the cylinder rotating, saw the noses of the slugs in the chambers, saw that he was a fraction of a second from death. To draw his gun when Trench was already covering him from just a few feet away was a desperate chance, and he knew it. He was weak, dizzy, and unsteady on his feet—not conditions conducive of a fast draw. Worst of all, with his senses dulled by heat and pain, he had lost track of how many rounds he had fired from the Colt. Had he shot six times, or only five? Even if he could draw before Trench killed him, the hammer of the Colt might fall on an empty chamber.

But men who are as good as dead have nothing to lose by trying, and Shannon was not the kind of man to surrender quietly, however heavy the odds against him. In desperation, he whipped the Colt out of the holster and pulled the trigger. The weapon bucked and roared, as the last cartridge discharged its lead into Hack Trench's body. Trench had also triggered his own six-gun, but Shannon's bullet struck him a millisecond before the hammer fell, and Trench's last shot merely kicked up a puff of dust next to Shannon's feet.

Trench dropped his six-gun, staggered to the edge of the boardwalk, and teetered there, holding his hands to his midsection and staring unbelievingly at Shannon.

"Blast you, Shannon," he gasped. "You've killed me. I hope you rot in . . ."

His voice failed, and his eyes glazed over. He toppled off the boardwalk, landing face first in the water trough that stood next to the boardwalk in front of the hotel. No bubbles came up through the water.

Shannon reholstered the empty Colt. He wanted to move forward, to get out of the street and the glare of the sun, but for some reason he couldn't will his legs to work. He looked up at the huge, glaring sun, and wondered vaguely why the entire town of Yellow Flats seemed to be spinning around so rapidly.

Then he fainted.

Chapter Twenty-one
Awakening

His first sensations were of pleasant semidarkness, of a blessed absence of pain, and of something wet and cold lying across his forehead.

Shannon looked around and realized that he was back in George Porter's spare room bed. Quickly the memories came flooding back to him, and he tried to sit up. A firm arm restrained him, pushing him back onto the pillows, and Shannon saw that the doctor was sitting by the bedside.

Still dazed, Shannon put his hand up and pulled away the wet cloth that was wrapped around his head.

"Take it easy, son," said the doctor, replacing the cloth on his forehead. "What brains you've got left are half-fried. It's a wonder you didn't die of heatstroke out there

238

on that roof. The next time you decide to wage a one-man war at high noon in the desert, at least wear a hat."

Shannon saw George Porter standing by the bed.

"Trench?" Shannon whispered.

"Dead, along with all of his gang," Porter said, grinning. "You did it, boy. You wiped them out."

"I left my rifle on the roof of the hotel," said Shannon fuzzily. "Could somebody get it for me?"

"I already did," Porter said, pointing to the corner where the Winchester was leaning.

"Thanks," Shannon said. "I'd hate to lose it. I may need it again sometime."

"That's enough talk for now," the doctor said. "Let's go, George. This man needs rest, and lots of it. Get some sleep, Marshal. You've earned it."

Shannon turned his face to the wall and slept.

The delegation arrived three days later. Shannon was sitting up in bed eagerly consuming some soup that Porter's housekeeper had prepared for him, when they came filing into the room, looking sheepish.

"Doc says you'll be up and about in a couple of days," the owner of the Green Lantern Saloon said. "Guess that leg's still pretty bad, though, isn't it?"

"He'll be limping for a while, if that's what you mean," said the doctor from the doorway. George Porter was with him.

"We came to give you the rest of your fee," the café

owner said. "Here it is—four hundred dollars." He dropped the money on the table beside the bed.

Shannon glanced at the money, then back at the men who stood in front of him, fidgeting nervously.

"No hurry about the fee," Shannon said. "There may still be some of Trench's gang around. I'll be back in the office tomorrow or the next day at the latest, and I'll make sure the job's finished before I take your money."

"The job *is* finished, as far as we're concerned," said the owner of the Rathole Saloon. "You kept your part of the bargain, and we're keeping ours. There's your money. You can go anytime."

"Still trying to run me out of town, gentlemen?" Shannon asked, raising an eyebrow.

"Well, I wouldn't put it quite that way," said the owner of the Green Lantern hastily. "It's just that, well, we don't want any more violence. All this killing is bad for business."

"The killing is what you hired me for," Shannon said. "Or had you forgotten?"

Annoyance showed on the saloon owner's face.

"We're just saying that you fulfilled the contract, and we're paying you off. You did the job, you got your money. No more arguments, Mr. Shannon, please. We've made up our minds. The town's tame now, and you're not needed here anymore. Besides, we can't afford to have a cripple for our marshal. Time for you to move on."

"Ah, I see," Shannon said. "No pensions for damaged town tamers. And who's going to be your guardian angel after I'm gone?"

"Oh, Joe Treadle can handle it from now on," the café owner said. "We appointed him town marshal this morning."

"How appropriate," Shannon said. "You deserve each other."

"Well," said the proprietor of the Green Lantern, "we'd better be getting back to our businesses. Don't suppose we'll be seeing you back this way again, Mr. Shannon, so we'll say good-bye now."

They shuffled out of the room, glancing apologetically at Porter and the doctor as they passed.

After they had left, Porter and the doctor came into the room.

"I'm sorry, Clay," George Porter said. "I told them what I thought of them, but it didn't make any difference. They really mean it this time—they want you gone."

"What a bunch of ungrateful hypocrites," said the doctor. "After what you did for them too."

"No, Doc," Shannon said, "they're right. We had an agreement. I kept my part of it, and they kept theirs. Now they want me to disappear, which is exactly what I expected when I took the job. I've got no complaints."

He swung his legs over the edge of the bed and stood up, wincing as he put his full weight on the injured leg.

"I'd stay in bed another day or two if I were you," the doctor warned. "You still aren't a hundred percent yet."

"No, I'd rather get dressed and be on my way," Shannon said. "That old buckskin stallion of mine must be getting fat and lazy by now. It'll do us both good to hit the trail again. So if you'll excuse me, gentlemen, I'll pack up and head for the livery stable. No use embarrassing Yellow Flats with my presence any longer than necessary."

He saddled the buckskin, added his saddlebags and bedroll to the horse's back, and mounted. Porter had come down to the livery stable to see him off.

"Are you going to be all right?" Porter asked. "You can barely walk."

"I'll let the horse do the walking," Shannon said. "He's better at it than I am right now."

"Don't forget your money," said Porter. "You left your four hundred dollars on the table in the bedroom." He held money out to Shannon.

"You and Doc split it," Shannon said. "I owe both of you for taking care of me when I was hurt."

"But it's yours," Porter said. "You certainly earned it."

"I don't want it," Shannon said. "It's hard to explain, but I just don't want those people's money."

He picked up the reins.

"Good-bye, George," he said. "Thanks for everything."

"Good-bye, Clay. Good luck."

Shannon turned the buckskin's head and started down the street toward the edge of town. It did not escape his notice that as he rode by, several residents of Yellow Flats paused to watch his passage with unfriendly eyes.

He rode past the splintered town limits sign and started along the trail out across the desert. A half mile outside Yellow Flats, he paused to look back. The town sat squatting in the desert, as small and sun-baked and ugly as when he had first seen it.

I've got to hand it to you, Cash, Shannon murmured. *You called the turn, all right. From the top of the world to the bottom of the heap. Well, hello, bottom. I think I've arrived.*

Then, crippled, unemployed, and alone, Clay Shannon turned his back on the town of Yellow Flats, and rode slowly away toward the line of hills on the western horizon.

Chapter Twenty-two
Epilogue

A week later he made camp in a low range of soft green hills, far away from Yellow Flats and the barren emptiness of the salt desert. There was water and firewood in the hills, and Shannon was grateful for both. Sipping a cup of hot coffee, he sat beside the campfire, staring into the flames and wondering what the future held for him—if anything.

The buckskin nickered softly, and Shannon realized that a horseman was approaching. He slipped the rawhide thong off the hammer of the Colt and waited.

"Hello, the camp!" cried a cheerful voice.

"Come on in if you're peaceful," Shannon replied.

A young man on a gray horse materialized out of the darkness, dismounted, and advanced toward the fire.

"Saw the fire and smelled the coffee," he said. "Can you spare a cup? I ran out a couple of days ago."

Shannon handed him the cup, noting as he did so that the young man wore a deputy sheriff's star on his shirt.

"You from around here?" Shannon asked as the deputy sat down by the fire.

"Naw, I been down south delivering a prisoner to Fort Grant," the deputy said. "My name's Reynolds. I work for Bob Hollister, the sheriff of Jackson County, up north of here."

"Hollister?" Shannon said. "Is that the same Bob Hollister who used to be marshal of Longhorn, Kansas?"

"The very same," Reynolds laughed. "Why? Do you know him?"

"Used to be his deputy in Longhorn," Shannon said. "Good man. You're lucky to be working with him."

"You still a lawman?" Reynolds asked.

"Not at the moment," Shannon replied. "Looking for a job, though."

"Bob thought a lot of the people he worked with in Longhorn," the deputy said. "Maybe he'd have something for you. Would you like to ride on up there with me and talk to him?"

"I wouldn't mind," Shannon said softly.

Bob Hollister's hair was gray now, but his eyes still twinkled as brightly as they had so long ago when he was Marshal of Longhorn and Shannon was his newest deputy. He rose from his desk and grasped Shannon's hand firmly in his own.

"It's been a lot of years, Clay," he said. "Great to see you. You look tired, though. Long trip?"

"Very long," Shannon said, sinking into a chair and stretching his aching leg out before him.

"Looks like you had a little bad luck," Hollister said, indicating the leg.

"Yeah," Shannon said. "Place called Yellow Flats. I forgot to duck."

"I suppose you heard about Cash Bonham," said Hollister somberly.

"About him being shot in the back and paralyzed? Yes, I took over from him in Cauldron County. But I also heard a few weeks ago that he was improving, getting back the use of his legs."

"He was," Hollister said, "but now he's dead."

"Dead?"

"Yes, he was almost fully recovered from that bullet in the back, so he took a job marshaling in some town near his brother's ranch. He shouldn't have done it, but he did. Guess he just couldn't stop being a lawman."

"What happened?"

"Some teenage hoodlum killed him. You know, one of the ones who want to make a quick reputation by gunning down somebody famous."

"Yes," Shannon said ruefully. "I've met a few of those myself."

"I guess we all have. Anyway, this one decided to

challenge Cash. Cash tried to take his gun away, but it came down to gunplay and the kid outdrew him. I never thought anybody, except maybe you, would ever outdraw Cash Bonham."

Well, Cash, Shannon thought, *I guess it really is twilight for the dinosaurs, isn't it? Rest in peace, my friend.*

"So, Clay," Hollister went on. "What brings you to Jackson County?"

"Looking for a job," Shannon said. "Met your man Reynolds on the trail and he suggested I talk to you."

Hollister frowned.

"Not much chance here, I'm afraid," he said. "Big county, small budget, not much action anymore. We're so civilized it's pathetic. Most of my people here at the county seat spend their time serving civil papers, and there's not even much demand for that these days. Anyway, the county's got me on a short leash, and I don't have the money to hire anybody else right now."

Shannon tried not to show his disappointment.

"I understand," he said. "Things seem to be that way all over these days."

"There is one possibility, though," Hollister continued, looking hard at Shannon. "It's not a very attractive proposition, but at least it's something."

"I don't have a lot of options right now," Shannon said. "I'm out of aces, as somebody told me not long ago. What's the job?"

"This county's so big that I have to put resident

deputies out in a couple of the outlying areas—permanent offices, single men on their own, no help, precious little pay, and no thanks at all. Ever hear of a place called Whiskey Creek?"

"Didn't they have a gold strike there about a year back?"

"Yeah, not a big one, but enough to attract a lot of people and a lot of trouble. The place is a real hole, no law to speak of, some rough folks running the place, you know how mining towns are. Normally I wouldn't worry about a mining camp much, except that the deputy I had stationed over there turned up dead awhile back, and I haven't been able to spare anybody to check into it yet."

"You think he was murdered?"

"Probably, but I can't say for sure. That's why I need someone to go over to Whiskey Creek, reopen the office there, and find out what happened to our man. Fifty dollars a month and expenses—when and if you can get the county to pay them. It's a pretty lousy situation, and I don't envy whoever takes it on, but if you want it, the job's yours."

"I want it," Shannon said.

Hollister reached into his desk drawer and withdrew a deputy sheriff's star.

"Stand up," he said, "and I'll swear you in."

The following morning, Deputy Sheriff Clay Shannon saddled the buckskin stallion and set out along the road to Whiskey Creek.

"Well, pal," Shannon said to the horse, "we've fallen about as far as we can, now. So what will this job turn out to be? A new beginning—or the end of the trail?"

The horse did not answer, so Shannon rode on, quietly hoping.

Dear Patron: You are i
or two, signed or
Your comments
selectio
a

A

Gloucester Library
P.O. Box 2380
Gloucester, VA 23061